DEFYING ITS CREATOR

Dr. Steiner immediately looked out the windshield.

More missiles and plasma shells hit Rex-1. Screaming in agony, the cyborg's legs buckled, and it fell against the Kremlin. The building crumbled, burying the cyber-beast under tons of rubble. A thick black cloud of dust flew into the air.

Silence.

Dr. Steiner's jaw dropped. *No! It can't be…*

Suddenly, two red lights flared in the dust cloud, glaring at the Nighthawk. Laser beams fired.

Instantly, the Nighthawk spiraled out of control. The screams of sirens and crewmembers mingled in Dr. Steiner's ears as inertia and vertigo slammed him against the wall. He forced his eyes open and watched through the windshield as the Moscow streets rushed up to them. There was an ear-shattering crash.

Everything went black.

DESTROYER
DELUXE EDITION

NATHAN MARCHAND
NATASHA HAYDEN
TIMOTHY DEAL
WITH
NICK HAYDEN

To: Kendallville Public Library,
May your patrons enjoy!

Matthew Marchand

This novella is dedicated to the tiny town of Story, Indiana, the wondrous place where this book was conceptualized.

CONTENTS

DESTROYER

DELUXE EDITION

PART 1
By Nathan Marchand

CHAPTER 1:
THE MEAT LOCKER

Icy air hissed through the door to the massive freezer as Eva tugged it open. Dr. Steiner saw goosebumps run down his daughter's arms as her sweat chilled. She buttoned up her lab coat, although it would provide little warmth. It always scared her when she went into the freezer, even with her father by her side. She simply couldn't quell the primal fear of the monster inside this old meat locker, even if the beast had been dead for millions of years.

Eva seemed to inhale four lungs' worth of air in one breath, smelling frozen flesh, yet hesitated to take a step. Dr. Steiner smiled and snuck his hammy hand over to hold hers. She turned and smiled back. Her sapphire eyes beamed at him.

She still looks like the golden-haired princess she was as a child, thought Dr. Steiner.

"You have nothing to fear," he told her in his slight German accent. He resisted the temptation to go into a scientific treatise on the unlikelihood of a creature surviving a 70 million-year slumber. She hated it when he did that. "Stop talking to me like a little girl," she'd say. "I have a Ph.D. now, too, remember?" So, he kept his mouth shut.

Feeling bolder, Eva let go of her father's hand and walked into the meat locker. Dr. Steiner followed.

The cold mist quickly dissipated, unveiling the beast's huge grin of exposed teeth around its giant maw, which could easily swallow a man. The eyes on top of its wedge-shaped head remained closed in its death-sleep, yet it still had a frightening glare even from behind sealed eyelids. Its skin was dark and scaly. The air was saturated with the smell of decay. As more mist cleared, the beast's outstretched 40-foot body was revealed, its tail resting against the wall.

The Steiners affectionately called him "Rex," which was short for Tyrannosaurus Rex.

Dr. Steiner walked to the sleeping giant's head and poked it several times.

Eva's fear melted into annoyance. "I get it, Dad," she said indignantly, putting her hands on her hips. "It's been dead since the Cretaceous period."

"Actually, I was pointing out where I wanted you to cut a skin sample with the laser cutter, *jah*," replied Dr. Steiner, grinning boyishly. It made him look like a mischievous high school kid instead of a graying old scientist.

Eva couldn't help but sigh to stifle a laugh. "What am I ever going to do with you, doctor?"

"I'd say, 'feed me to the beastie,' but I wouldn't want to wake Rex. He's probably cranky in the morning."

"You little..." said Eva, shaking her head.

Dr. Steiner just kept grinning.

Composing herself, Eva reached into one of her lab coat pockets and produced a laser cutter the size of a pen. Dr. Steiner reached into his own pocket for a pair of latex gloves, which he put on, and a plastic bag. Eva stepped toward the dinosaur's corpse and, with the press of a button on the laser cutter, sliced a one-inch square piece of skin from the spot her father had poked. It sizzled like bacon being fried; it smelled like it, too. Once it was cut, Dr. Steiner carefully removed the ancient flesh from the frozen hide and sealed it inside the plastic bag. He then placed the bag in his lab coat's breast pocket.

"And he didn't so much as twitch," said Dr. Steiner.

Eva simply rolled her eyes at his teasing. "I hope he wakes up and eats you."

Dr. Steiner laughed. Eva joined him a second later.

"All right, enough joking around," said Dr. Steiner. "Let's examine this skin sample. I want to see if the newest batch of microbots can reanimate this dead tissue."

Eva nodded in agreement. "Good. If I stay in here much longer, I'll catch a million-year-old strain of the flu."

Father and daughter walked toward the door in the ice-blue wall. Eva resisted the temptation to look back to see if "Rex" was following them; she wanted to avoid any more teasing. It amused her father.

They exited the freezer only to be met by the cold looks of two men in military uniforms standing in the middle of the lab.

CHAPTER 2:
OF MEN AND MONSTERS

The two soldiers wore the same gray American Alliance Army dress uniforms, but they were both very different men.

The first was a tall gorilla of a man with specks of gray in the dark hair under his beret, which bore a single silver star. He had a chiseled face and a dented chin. Medals and lapels made of every precious metal on the Periodic Table were pinned on his chest, the most prominent being the eagle and shield insignia of the Alliance Army. It was a wonder he didn't collapse under the weight.

The other man was a flagpole by comparison. He was a gaunt man with receding brown hair and a softer face. He nervously pushed a pair of thick, old-fashioned spectacles up the bridge of his nose with a thin hand. No medals adorned his uniform except for a crucifix hanging from his neck. A small Bible did peek out of his breast pocket. White cross insignias were stitched onto both of his shoulders.

"Doctor Kiefer Steiner, I presume," said the first soldier in a voice that could command a god.

"You presume correctly, General Gunn," replied Dr. Steiner. He glanced at Eva and motioned her to close the meat locker. She did so as her father continued to talk to the general.

Dr. Steiner walked to Gunn and shook his hand.

"This is Father Daniels, the Army's head chaplain," said Gunn, motioning to the other soldier.

"Pleased to meet you, doctor," said the chaplain meekly, nodding politely.

"The feeling is mutual, padre," replied Dr. Steiner, shaking Daniels' hand. He turned back to the general. "I didn't know you were a religious man."

"I'm not, but Daniels has been my trusted advisor for ten years. I appreciate his wisdom regardless of his spiritual beliefs, especially in these trying times."

"Thank you, sir," injected Daniels.

"I take it she is your daughter?" inquired Gunn, pointing behind Dr. Steiner.

The doctor glanced over to see Eva come up and stand next to him.

"Yes, I'm the other 'Doctor Steiner' in the family," said Eva.

Her father smiled at her beaming confidence, but quickly turned to his unexpected guests. "What brings you to a humble scientist's lab, *herr* Gunn?"

Gunn's expression became very grave. "We need your help to end the war."

Dr. Steiner was taken aback, but he tried hard to swallow Gunn's bombshell. Eva's eyes were wide as plates in shock.

After a few seconds of dead silence, Dr. Steiner finally spoke. "Would you gentlemen care to discuss this upstairs?"

"That would be fine, doctor," said Gunn.

A pair of scientists and a pair of military men sat across from each other on two sofas. A metal kettle of steaming coffee sat on the table between them. Eva poured herself a cup—her third one that day—and gave one cup to her father. She offered some to Gunn and Daniels, but they turned her down.

"You're a difficult man to contact," Gunn said to Dr. Steiner.

"I've been busy with my latest discovery," replied the doctor after taking a sip of his coffee.

"The T-Rex corpse you discovered?" asked Gunn.

"Yes. I found it in a cave lined with a strange element that's been giving my mineralogist friends a heyday. It was completely unlike anything on Earth, so we concluded it was extraterrestrial in origin. It was probably deposited in the cave during a meteor shower millions—if not billions—of years ago. The T-Rex probably wandered into the cave and was trapped during a cave-in, after which it most likely starved to death. But the alien radiation from this element preserved the creature's body in near perfect condition from the moment of death."

"I find it strange that a cyberneticist would want to examine a dinosaur corpse."

"Paleontology is one of my hobbies."

"Besides," added Eva, sipping her coffee, "it gives him a chance to use his microbots to help me examine the creature's cellular structure. I'm writing my second doctorate dissertation on this research."

Dr. Steiner grinned. Hearing Eva talk about her research always made him proud of her.

"But I doubt scientific research is why you're here," said Dr. Steiner, placing his hot cup on the table.

"No, we came here to beseech you to end the madness devouring this world's soul," said Father Daniels ominously.

Clank! Eva slammed her cup on the table. "You came here to ask my father to make you a weapon?" She seemed to forget her father was sitting next to her. "You military types are all the same. You have no interest in science unless it helps you blow up more people faster."

"Miss Steiner, I have seen this mad war firsthand," said Father Daniels, shuttering. His voice seemed to shiver. "I have read countless young men their last rites while under the scream of gunfire—seeing so much death will chill your very soul. The Russo-Chinese Coalition must be stopped. I beg you to understand."

Anger contorted Eva's face. She pointed at the chaplain. "My father—
"

"—can speak for himself," injected Dr. Steiner, lowering Eva's hand with his own. He told her to calm down with a glance, something he had done with her since childhood. She obeyed.

He turned to Gunn. "I have lost two sons in this long war…" His voice was grave. "What is your proposal?"

Eva gasped, her eyes wide.

Gen. Gunn leaned forward slightly. "You are the world's leading authority on cybernetics. The Alliance Army wants you to create a cyber-weapon for us."

"Why not use nuclear weapons?"

"We want to end the war, not destroy the world."

Dr. Steiner paused to consider. The silence was deafening.

"I will not do human experimentation, whether the subjects are living or dead. I refuse to maim anyone, no matter how good the cause. I am not a mad scientist."

"Understood," replied Gen. Gunn, nodding.

"In which case, I must be in charge of the project. I will not allow any ethically dubious work to be done."

Gen. Gunn nodded again.

"If the Army isn't willing to abide by my terms, I suggest you take your proposal elsewhere."

Eva's angry expression melted slightly. It didn't last long.

"The Army will not only agree to your terms, it will spare none of its resources so you can complete your work."

Dr. Steiner glanced at Eva, who gave him a disapproving stare. He looked away, eyes closed, deep in thought. He needed to give an answer quickly. *This is for the greater good.*

Dr. Steiner straightened himself, looked Gen. Gunn in the eye, and said, "Then you will have your weapon."

Eva buried her face in her hands.

Gen. Gunn shook Dr. Steiner's hand. "You are a patriot, good doctor. I will contact you in several days to begin preparations."

Father Daniels also shook the doctor's hand. "May the Lord bless your efforts." He clutched the large cross dangling from his neck.

The military men were gone within a minute.

Only then did Eva look up to break her silence. "You damn fool! You sold out!"

Dr. Steiner crinkled his forehead. "This is for the good of our country, Eva, for the whole world."

"No, it's not. They're not interested in your discovery or the potential of your inventions. They just want you to make them a bigger gun."

"The purpose of science—"

"Don't lecture me! What's to stop them from perverting anything you make for them? You know that's what always happens when the military gets their hands any new invention. You may end this war, but you'll end up starting the next one. And then there may not be anyone left to start another one."

"That's why I want you on this project with me. You can be its conscience."

Eva stood and took several steps toward the lab's door, her back to her father. "I'll work on this project, but it's not what needs a conscience—*you are*." With that, she disappeared through the door.

Dr. Steiner sighed, picking up his now cold cup and sipped its equally cold contents. It was chalky brown ice water. He gagged down a mouthful and put the cup down. He hated cold coffee. But he hated having his daughter angry at him even more. Who could blame her, though? This wasn't the first time men in uniforms had come to them asking for them to weaponize their latest technological breakthroughs. She was tired of people seeing only barbaric applications for them.

Most of all, though, Eva knew her history. Just 150 years earlier, the government turned to a select group of scientists in the Manhattan Project to create a superweapon—the atomic bomb—before its enemies did, all in the name of ending another destructive war. It succeeded, but at the price of thousands of lives and decades of political tension. The end of the world was only a button press away. Now, with metagenetics—her field of study—and cybernetics booming and with another war raging, the military was again looking for a silver bullet to kill the latest monster it was fighting.

Eva refused to create another atomic bomb.

Dr. Steiner picked up the kettle and his cup and walked to the kitchen. He put the kettle on the hydrostove and dumped the cold coffee down the drain. Then he sat in a chair at the kitchen table. He rested his chin on his hand. *I have the power to bring peace to a war-ravaged world. I can't sit by and do nothing. My conscience will not allow it. For the sake of the future, I will end this war.*

CHAPTER 3:
APOLLYON

One year later...

"Please let the general through," said Dr. Steiner.

Security at Site Alpha made Fort Knox look like a tourist trap. Even allowing military brass required Dr. Steiner's approval. It was one of the concessions he was given so he could make sure there was no "funny business" happening on this project. It even made Eva more willing to work on it.

But in this case, Dr. Steiner simply wanted to greet his guests himself.

The guard pressed a button and the door before the doctor and Eva whirred open. Gen. Gunn and Father Daniels stood before them along with a young Japanese man wearing an American Alliance Air Force uniform. He looked to be fresh out of the Academy, with bright catlike eyes and an eager smile that made him look like a spokesman for toothpaste. He took one look at Eva and produced a comb—such an archaic device—from his pocket and ran it through his jet black hair. Eva flared her nostrils, hoping to hide her annoyance. She failed.

"*Hallo*, and welcome to Site Alpha, general," said Dr. Steiner, shaking Gunn's hand.

"Or as our team likes to call it, 'Monster Island,'" added Eva.

"Sounds like they've been cooped up here a little too long," said Gunn, laughing. He motioned to the young Japanese man, who was shooting Eva coy glances. "This is Private Tomoyuki Yamamoto, the pilot you requested."

"Call me 'Tomo,'" he said, bowing slightly. "That goes double for you, Goldie Locks," he said to Eva as he looked up, grinning ear-to-ear. "I've always had a weakness for blondes."

"Nice try, flyboy," retorted Eva tersely.

"Can't blame a guy for trying, right?"

Dr. Steiner cleared his throat loudly, then said, "Thank you for coming, general. Your superiors will be pleased to know the project is ahead of schedule."

Father Daniels sighed. "It seems God's ear has been attentive to the cries of his people on the battlefield and will soon bring them deliverance."

"The sooner, the better," said Gunn. "We just lost three provinces to the Coalition this week. At this rate, we'll lose half of Europe in a few months. They'll conquer the continent within a year."

Father Daniels clutched his crucifix, mumbling a prayer. Tomo just kept grinning.

"Then let me show you what we've 'cooked up' in the lab," said Dr. Steiner, rubbing his hands.

He led the group to the opposite wall where there was a door bearing large red letters that said, "HANGER 1." The guard pressed a button and the door parted, ushering them into a gigantic room filled with rushing scientists and workers. The sauna-like humidity made all their clothes stick to their skin while their noses inhaled stale air that was filled the smell of burning fuel. Fluorescent light beamed down from the ceiling. Within a few steps, all three of Dr. Steiner's guests stopped dead in their tracks, staring up at steep angles, but it wasn't to find the high cathedral-like ceiling.

It was to see the monster.

Towering over them thanks to countless hydraulic braces stood a metal body over a hundred feet tall. Its thick legs and clawed feet were covered with slate-gray exo-armor. The armor ascended half-way up the torso, leaving a jagged ribcage and broad shoulder bones exposed. A left arm dangled from its shoulder while a robotic crane lifted a right arm to the other socket. Jutting out of the metallic monstrosity's back were bones shaped like wings. Sparks fell like hot rain as a dozen workers hanging from titanium-fiber cables welded exo-armor onto exposed circuitry. Other workers were installing various computer components within the skeleton. It was like watching a giant form outside of its mother's womb.

Gunn's eyes widened. Tomo was in awe. Daniels reflexively crossed himself.

"Meet Rex-1," said Dr. Steiner, "my greatest creation."

After a few seconds, Tomo's awe melted into laughter. "*Konichiwa*, Sexy Rexy!" he said, waving at the giant robot.

Eva frowned at his cheekiness.

Gunn spoke next. "This is the weapon you've been working on?"

Dr. Steiner crossed his arms and nodded, grinning like a proud father.

Gunn wasn't amused. "It's a giant dinosaur model kit!"

"I prefer the term 'walking weapons platform.'"

"And it's not a dinosaur," added Eva matter-of-factly. "It's a dragon."

Gunn shot Dr. Steiner a bewildered glance. "Why a dragon?"

"Psychological warfare, general. Dragons exist in almost every culture's mythology. They are a universal symbol of dread and terror. People see them as treasure hoarders, killers, and maiden-nappers. The Coalition will either cower at the first site of our titanium titan or fear it after it destroys their army."

Eva hid her disappointment under a veil of stoicism as she listened to her father's proud words.

"You call it a 'weapons platform,'" said Gunn. "What is it armed with?"

"Once operational, it will carry fifty Warhawk missiles, a hundred Stinger-5 missiles, and, if necessary, one nuclear warhead. For defense, we'll be installing a state-of-the-art energy shield, which should be able to absorb most attacks. All of this is powered by a cold fusion reactor the size of a baseball in its chest."

"Whoa," injected Tomo, looking like a boy admiring a toy he could never have.

"The head will also be equipped with a pair of lasers and a flamethrower."

"Where is the head?" asked Gunn.

"Ah," said Dr. Steiner, motioning his guests to follow him, "come with me."

Gunn and Tomo immediately stepped toward Dr. Steiner and Eva, but not the chaplain. Gunn looked back. Daniels' eyes were still locked on Rex-1. The man's skin glistened, his breathing quickened. It was as if the huge machine had a supernatural grip on him.

"Padre!" called Gunn.

Daniels snapped out of his trance. "Yes, general?"

"Hurry up."

Daniels nodded, wiping sweat from his brow, and quickly followed.

Dr. Steiner led the group to a large door near the corner of the hangar. Behind the door was a corridor wide enough to drive three tanks side-by-side through. A hundred feet down the corridor was another gate-like door, which opened automatically as the doctor and his guests approached it.

Daniels gasped at what he saw.

A wedge-shaped metal head the size of a bus grinned at them like a crocodile. Razor teeth lined its maw, which was big enough to swallow a car. A pair of cannon-like holes protruded from its snout. Crimson light reflected from the laser lenses in its eyes as it seemed to stare at the humans. A crown of horns circled its face. Sparks flared as several workers welded armor plating along its jawline.

Tomo, as usual, was elated.

Daniels was paralyzed. His face resembled the screaming man in an Edvard Munch painting. The only movement he made was his trembling lower lip.

As if forgetting the monstrous head, Gunn turned immediately to the chaplain. "Daniels, what's wrong?"

Terror loosened its grip on Daniels, just enough for his quaking voice to speak. "'And they had a king over them, which is the angel of the bottomless pit, whose name in the Hebrew tongue is Abaddon, but in the Greek tongue hath his name...'" He shuttered slightly. "'Apollyon.'"

"Apollyon?" said Gunn, perplexed.

11

"It means 'Destroyer,'" said Eva gravely. "According to the Bible, he is a demon who will lead a plague of locusts against mankind during the end of the world."

Even Tomo's expression became serious hearing that.

"Daniels!" barked Gunn, grabbing the chaplain's shoulders and shaking him. "Snap out of it!"

Daniels jerked like he had been awakened from sleepwalking. He took several deep breaths. "I'm sorry, sir."

Gunn released Daniels and turned back to Dr. Steiner. "You were saying?"

Despite his misgivings about the general's nonchalant handling of the situation, Dr. Steiner went back to his explanation: "We're working on Rex-1's head separately because it is the key to the whole project."

He led them up a flight of stairs and into an observation deck. A window stretching the entire length of the 20-foot room overlooked the huge head. Three technicians supervised the many blinking and *bleeping* computers around them.

Followed by his guests, Dr. Steiner walked to a monitor near the center of the observation window and pressed a button. A three-dimensional schematic of Rex-1's head appeared on the screen. Dr. Steiner pressed a few more buttons, highlighting a large area inside the head.

"Rex-1 is wired with computer technology so advanced, it was considered science fiction just a few decades ago," began Dr. Steiner. "But its CPU is actually something far more advanced than even that."

"Your mom?" injected Tomo, snickering.

Dr. Steiner shot him an annoyed glance. "Young man, that joke is older than the dinosaurs. In fact, I think it was unearthed with the first dinosaur fossils found over 200 years ago."

Tomo crossed his arms and harrumphed.

Dr. Steiner continued: "No, a biological brain."

"A brain?" said Gunn.

"*Jah*, a T-Rex brain, to be exact. I used microbots to extract brain cells from the T-Rex corpse I discovered. I then used the microbots to regenerate the brain to serve as a bio-computer for Rex-1."

"You cloned the brain," said Gunn.

"*Jah*, but I also re-engineered it to fit our purposes."

"But why a brain?"

"No matter how advanced our machines become, they still cannot compare to the computing power of a living brain. Brain cells handle thousands of operations, both conscious and unconscious, per minute, performing tasks with precision no machine can rival, even now. A robot—a cyborg, really—this advanced requires a computer capable of performing millions of complex operations. A bio-computer was the best option."

"Don't tell me you're going to allow this dinosaur brain to run the cyborg on its own?"

"Certainly not," replied Dr. Steiner, shaking his head. "Let me show you something." He motioned everyone to follow him again.

Dr. Steiner walked to a chair in the center of the room. In the chair was a device that looked like an old motorcycle helmet with wires attached to a computer next to it. He picked up the helmet and displayed it for all to see.

"Recently, the Air Force began working on a project called 'T.P. Pilot.'"

"Toilet paper pilot?" interrupted Tomo. "Sounds like a weird prank."

"It means 'telepathic pilot,'" retorted Eva, clearly annoyed.

"The aim was to create a device that could allow a pilot to control an aircraft with his thoughts," continued Dr. Steiner. "This helmet was the fruit of that project." He put it on. "A pilot wears this and his thoughts are transmitted to the aircraft—or in our case, the cyborg—without having to be onboard the craft. Its range is limited, however. Five miles, at the most."

"Incredible!"

"Well said, Tomo, especially since you will be the pilot."

"Really?"

Dr. Steiner nodded, taking off the helmet and handing it to him.

Tomo pumped his fist, exclaiming, "Yes!" He sat in the chair and tried the helmet on. It was a little big on his head, but it didn't damper his excitement.

"You'll start simulations soon," Dr. Steiner told him.

Dr. Steiner turned to Gunn. "There you have it, general. Does it look like your investment is paying off?"

"It does," he replied, nodding. "When will it be ready?"

"In six months. A year at the latest."

"Make it sooner than later, doctor," said Gunn, his voice suddenly firmer. "Time, among other things, is on the Coalition's side. We can't afford to surrender. I expect a good report from you in six months. Good day."

"*Auf wiedersehen*, general."

Gunn called Tomo and Daniels and told them it was time to leave. Tomo reluctantly removed the helmet and placed it back on the chair. He said, "*Sayonara*," to Eva, wearing a huge grin. Daniels clutched his crucifix, muttering prayers in Latin. Then the three soldiers left the room.

"It seems they all liked your new baby," Eva said to her father after the soldiers departed. "I hope you're happy."

13

Dr. Steiner tried to take hold of his daughter's hand, but she shook him off. He swallowed his anger.

"Rex-1 isn't a monster—it's a peacemaker."

"It's a weapon."

"A weapon that will end a terrible war. If your brothers were still alive, they would understand."

"Don't bring them into this."

"Why not?"

"Because I don't want you perverting your science in order to make a weapon in their names."

Dr. Steiner looked away for a second to avoid losing his temper. "You know I'm doing the right thing."

"We'll find out in six months."

She walked away, leaving her father alone in the middle of the busy room.

Dr. Steiner hung his head, sighed, and pounded the chair's armrest. *Why won't she understand?* He looked over at the gigantic head: his greatest achievement, yet his daughter hated it. It was a technological marvel that would not only end a war but advance dozens of scientific areas by leaps and bounds, and Eva wouldn't touch it with a ten-foot pole when she wasn't working on it. Was it because she distrusted the military? Or him? Was she angry that it had consumed much of the last year of his life? Didn't she see the cyborg's necessity?

I've come too far to back out now. My creation will fulfill its purpose.

CHAPTER 4:
THE BEAST FROM THE SEA

Six months later…

It was a cloudy day.

Dr. Steiner watched through the windshield as the murky gray veil split open upon the nose of the aircraft. The equally gray Baltic Sea stretched out before them. Small white crests jumped from the water as the light wind blew.

Descending was a risk. They were smack dab in the middle of Coalition territory. Just 200 miles behind them were the Coalition provinces formerly known as Norway and Sweden. Another 200 miles ahead was the coastline of Mother Russia, one of the seats of the Coalition. The only reason they were there was because their VTAL airplane was equipped with the most top secret of stealth technology.

Now I know why this thing's called a Nighthawk, thought Dr. Steiner.

Strapped in chairs throughout the strangely spacious cockpit were Eva, Gunn, Daniels, Tomo, and two Alliance Air Force pilots. Tomo sat near the pilots. He had a TP helmet in his lap and an excited grin on his face. Eva and Dr. Steiner were seated on the left side of the cockpit by several computer monitors that were in "stand by" mode, both wearing serious expressions, especially Eva. Gunn and Daniels sat toward the back. Gunn swiveled a mini-monitor from his armrest over his lap to overlook the operation. Daniels bent his head and muttered some prayers.

"We're approaching the coordinates, sir," reported one of the pilots, glancing over his shoulder at Gunn.

"Good work, O'Brian." He tapped the touchpad on his mini-monitor. "Descend to fifteen-hundred feet and maintain position."

"Yes, sir."

They felt the Nighthawk slow as the plane's nearly silent engines rotated into a hover position. They descended.

"Someone finally tell me why we're in the middle of a Coalition firing range," said Tomo, "that way I'll know what I died for."

"The details of this operation are on a strictly need-to-know basis," replied Gunn without taking his eyes off the monitor.

"I'm only the *kaiju's* pilot. I think I have a 'need-to-know basis.'"

"You also have a big mouth," said Gunn.

"It makes up for my small stature. So what?"

"Shut up, and you'll know what we're doing in a few minutes."

Tomo crossed his arms and sat back in his chair, an annoyed look on his face.

The Nighthawk lurched slightly as it stopped at an altitude of 1,500 feet.

"Hey, Tomo," said Eva.

Tomo was surprised and delighted to hear the blonde speaking to him. He turned to her wearing a big flirtatious smile.

Eva shot him a quick scowl, then asked, "What's a '*kaiju*'?"

Tomo snickered. "'*Kaiju*' is the Japanese word for 'monster.' You'd know this if you ever watched my country's old creature features in the original Japanese."

"Right…"

Eva turned back to her monitor.

Tomo grimaced in disappointment.

A few seconds later, he had a new question: "If we're here to find Rex-1—which I assume is the plan—but it was too big to airlift and it's too far for it to fly, how is it supposed to get here?"

Dr. Steiner finally spoke up. "The only other way we could get it here undetected."

"*Nani?*"

"*Charybdis* rising!" announced O'Brian.

Gunn punched a few buttons and activated everyone's monitors. It showed the sea below them as a huge metal object jutted from it. Water splattered against it and foamed around it as it rose. In five seconds, something the size of an aircraft carrier rested atop the waters.

"A submarine!" exclaimed Tomo.

"Point out the obvious," muttered Eva.

Dr. Steiner stifled a laugh.

"Enjoy it while you see it," said Gunn. "Our operation is the only thing more top secret than that sub."

Tomo's jaw hung open. "I think I'm in love."

"You're such a geek!" said Eva.

"*Arigato*," replied Tomo, still staring at the sub on his mini-monitor.

Eva cursed under her breath.

Dr. Steiner smiled in amusement.

Gunn pressed a few buttons and then looked over at Dr. Steiner. "Would you like to give the word, doctor? It is your creation, after all."

Dr. Steiner turned to him and said, "I'd be honored."

Gunn gestured for him to do so.

Dr. Steiner punched a button to open a radio channel to the *Charybdis*. "Rex-1…launch!"

The deck of the *Charybdis* split open. A silhouette slowly rose from underneath the launch bay doors. Even in the darkened sunlight, the giant's blood-red body shined. It was draped in what looked like a cape.

16

No discernible body parts could be seen aside from a long slender tail and a pair of four-toed feet with curved claws.

Finally, it finished its ascent, towering over 150 feet above the deck.

Awed silence flooded the cockpit.

Presently, the "cape" flew back—it was actually a pair of bat-like wings. They folded behind the robot's back, revealing the now completed body Dr. Steiner had shown to his Army friends just months before. Crimson scales covered it like armor. Arms ending with hands with four claws each rested at its sides. Canine teeth were exposed in its lipless maw, making it look like it was smiling. Glassy, lidless spheres were its eyes. The crown of six horns circling its head shined even on the cloudy day.

"IT'S ALIVE! IT'S ALIVE!"

Everyone in the cockpit—except Daniels, who stared at his monitor—fired a glare at Tomo.

He just grinned coyly. "Couldn't resist."

"I see you've grafted skin to its hull, doctor," said Gunn, looking at his monitor.

"It was a last minute addition, more for aesthetics than anything else. We used skin cloned from the T-Rex corpse. It makes it look more like a living, breathing dragon," replied the doctor.

Gunn turned toward Dr. Steiner, but paused when he saw Daniels still staring at his monitor, his hands trembling. "Padre…?"

"'And I stood upon the sand of the sea, and saw a beast rise up out of the sea, having seven heads and ten horns, and upon his horns ten crowns, and upon his heads the name of blasphemy.'"

Daniels suddenly swung his head toward Gunn. His eyes were wide and wild with fear, like he had seen the Grim Reaper. Gunn felt something a veteran soldier like him rarely experienced: a chill down his spine.

"Pray your monster does not bite the hand that feeds it," whispered Daniels, his tone more than foreboding. "It is damnation made flesh. May it strike only our enemies."

His gaze slowly returned to the monitor. He was clutching the crucifix around his neck tighter than ever.

Gunn wanted to say something, but now was not the right time or place. *I'm sorry, old friend.*

He looked past Daniels. "Doctor, this is your show now. I'm only here to supervise."

Dr. Steiner nodded.

Looking at each person he was addressing, he said, "Eva, bring up Rex-1's vitals for monitoring. Tomo, put on that TP helmet. I'll be patching you into Rex-1 shortly. O'Brian and Willis, set course for Moscow."

"I've been waiting for this moment for six months," said Tomo, putting on the TP helmet.

Dr. Steiner punched buttons to prepare for Tomo's link to Rex-1. Eva leaned toward her father and whispered, "We're going to Moscow?"

"Gunn didn't brief you, did he?" Dr. Steiner whispered.

Eva shook her head.

"We're going to strike at the enemy's heart by attacking one of the Coalition's capitals."

"Please tell me you're only attacking the Putin Military Base."

Dr. Steiner paused in his work. "*Herr*-Gunn told me that is the plan."

Eva looked away and pressed a button on her computer, bringing up a readout of Rex-1's vital systems. "I hope you're right," she said, not looking at her father. Her tone didn't sound hopeful.

Dr. Steiner sighed, and then redirected his attention back to the computer. He flipped a few more switches, the words Activate TP helmet? appearing on his monitor. He put his finger on another button. "Are you ready, Tomo?" he asked, looking over his shoulder.

"*Hai!*" shouted Tomo, giving a thumbs up.

"There will probably be some disorientation at first, but it will subside once your brain synchs with Rex-1's biological CPU."

"No problem!"

"Activating!" He pressed the button.

"OH YEAH!"

Instantly, Rex-1's eyes flared red. The giant cyborg bobbed its head as if to get kinks out of its neck. Then it threw back its head, mouth gaping, and bellowed a guttural roar that rattled the Nighthawk's hull.

Dr. Steiner glanced at Tomo. The young man had a look of terrified excitement, like he was riding a roller coaster. "How are you doing, Tomo?"

Tomo bellowed a long "Woo!"

"He's fine," muttered Dr. Steiner. He turned to Eva. "How are their vitals?"

"All systems go."

Dr. Steiner turned to O'Brian. "Take us to an altitude of 15,000 feet. That should hide us from their radar." He looked at Rex-1's pilot. "Got that, Tomo?"

"*Hai!*"

"Then it's off to Moscow!" exclaimed Gunn.

Tomo grunted, and Dr. Steiner looked at his monitor. Rex-1 growled, spread its leathery wings, and leapt from the *Charybdis'* deck. It skimmed the ocean, but after a few more flaps, it was soaring toward the Nighthawk. The aircraft's engines rumbled quietly as it ascended back to the clouds, the crimson titan of terror flying just behind them.

CHAPTER 5:
DEATH MACHINE

The dome-like spires of Moscow looked like a child's building blocks in the distance. They had flown for over fours hours, dodging the Coalition's air force and radar. Tomo had no problems ordering a flying cybernetic dinosaur around. He even cracked jokes about making "Jurassic Park, Part 13." It lightened an otherwise somber flight.

Daniels raised his hands above his head and started rattling off a prayer in Latin.

"What's he saying?" Dr. Steiner asked Gunn.

"I think it has something to do with God protecting us from our little demon and plucking our damned souls out of the pits of Hell should we die."

Dr. Steiner looked away, uneasy. "Sorry I asked."

"Approaching target," reported Willis. "ETA: one minute."

"Yamamoto, activate Rex-1's weapons!" ordered Gunn.

"With pleasure, sir!" replied Tomo. He closed his eyes and crinkled his forehead.

The weapons' readouts appeared on Dr. Steiner and Eva's monitors. Dr. Steiner punched a few buttons and replaced his readouts with a view of Rex-1 from the Nighthawk's outside camera. Eva hung her head, staring at the keyboard. Dr. Steiner sighed, and gently squeezed her shoulder. She glanced at him briefly, but turned away when her computer buzzed.

"ETA: thirty seconds," reported Willis.

They were almost over the Putin Military Base, one of the brains of the Coalition's fighting forces. Squads of aircraft were lined up in nice rows along airstrips. Tanks rolled across fields like remote-controlled toys. Soldiers looked like barely visible ants scampering about their concrete anthill.

"Enough hiding. Commence attack!" ordered Gunn.

"BANZAI!" shouted Tomo.

Dr. Steiner was glued to his monitor.

Rex-1 barrel-rolled into a steep dive. It folded its wings over its back, piercing the air like a bullet. The Nighthawk dove to follow it, but even it couldn't keep up. The monster stayed ahead of them, and within fifteen seconds, it spread its wings to slow its fall, landing on the airstrip in a thunderous cloud of dust. The Nighthawk maintained an altitude of 1,000 feet.

For several unending seconds, there was silence, shock, and awe. It was as if a god had fallen to Earth.

Suddenly, Rex-1 raised its head and roared—a warcry. Then it spat an inferno on a squad of warplanes. They erupted in flames.

"Shield up!" Gunn barked at Tomo.

It was perfect timing, for Coalition tanks quickly retaliated with a barrage of plasma shells. They exploded on contact. Rex-1 felt nothing as the energy shield flared with each impact. The cyborg glared at the tanks—the toys—with burning eyes. Instantly, its crown of horns glowed and red lasers shot from its eyes, and with one quick turn of its head, it sliced six tanks in half. They exploded in succession. Then Rex-1 turned to the airstrip's control tower, torched it, and swatted it with its claw.

"Incredible!" muttered Dr. Steiner. He glanced at Eva's computer. She beat him to his question and said, "Vitals are stable. There are a few minor spikes in its brain activity, but nothing to worry about."

"It's better than I imagined," said Dr. Steiner. He was in awe, even from watching at a distance. His ultimate creation, a culmination of his life's work, was raining punishment upon his nation's enemies. Pride swelled within him. He almost wished he was wearing the TP helmet, to experience the rush of the cyborg's battle. Almost.

Rex-1 crouched, and then it leapt 300 feet, landing on a hangar, crumbling it instantly. Its claws tore through the roof of the next hangar like it was made of paper. Green dots ran out of the hangar like frightened insects. Rex-1 plucked a Neo-MIG in each hand. It tossed them into other hangars like toys. Jet fuel ignited on impact. Rex-1 then grabbed a tank and pitched it across the airstrip at a squad of tanks heading for it. They scattered like pins hit by a bowling ball. Finally, Rex-1 breathed flames onto the remains of the hangars before it.

"Burn, baby, burn!" exclaimed Tomo. He acted like he was playing a virtual reality game.

Eva rested her elbows on the console and buried her face in her hands.

Dr. Steiner only sat there, unsure of what to say.

"'And there came down from heaven fire, and consumed him and his fifty!'" cried Daniels.

"Padre, control yourself!" ordered Gunn.

"Forgive me for my outburst, sir."

Gunn turned to Tomo. "What's the destruction rate of the base?"

Tomo broke his concentration slightly and replied, "Thirty-five percent,   sir."

"Finish it," Gunn commanded.

"*Hai!*" He closed his eyes to focus again.

Rex-1 unfurled its wings and took flight with three big gusts. It started circling the base a like giant vulture, just a few hundred feet in the sky. It unleashed one long fiery breath after another on the remaining buildings.

Fuel tanks exploded in pillars of fire. Retreating jeeps became rolling comets. Armored vehicles melted. Soldiers disappeared in explosions.

In two minutes, Putin Military Base was Hell on Earth.

At last, Rex-1 landed in the middle of the scorched airstrip as the base blazed. It folded its wings and stood erect, awaiting new orders. Amidst the red-orange aura of the flames, it looked like an apathetic demon overlooking the souls it tormented in the underworld. Only its crimson eyes burned brighter than its destructive handiwork.

"The base has been completely destroyed," reported Tomo, breathing heavy and sweating.

It was the understatement of the century. Everyone except Eva was glued to the site below them, silent. An inferno over a mile long. What was once a central hub of the Coalition's seemingly unstoppable armies was gone, destroyed in less than ten minutes. And there in the middle of it was the manmade god of wrath who had done it. It was a wonder—a terrifying wonder—to behold.

Dr. Steiner broke the silence. "All right…let's ask the Coalition for a surrender."

Eva peeked through her finders and glanced at her father. She seemed relieved.

Gunn paused in his reply, his hand on his chin. "No."

Dr. Steiner's eyes widened. Eva sat up and fired the general a shocked glare. Even Tomo seemed surprised. Daniels immediately crossed himself and muttered more prayers in Latin.

"What? We've beaten them, broken the back of their military power," said Dr. Steiner.

"No, only half," replied Gunn.

"The Chinese front won't dare oppose us after seeing what Rex-1 did here."

"They won't surrender, not unless we truly break them."

"What are you talking about?"

"The Japanese didn't surrender even after the first A-bomb was dropped. It took a second one for them to realize the Allies meant business. The Coalition is no different. They'll fight us to the last man unless we prove we have the power to destroy them completely." He turned to Tomo. "Yamamoto, fly Rex-1 southeast, straight to the Kremlin."

Eva gasped. "You're mad!"

Gunn looked at her with narrowing eyes. "No, I'm doing my job."

Eva turned to Dr. Steiner. "Dad, stop him."

He only sat there in silence, as if in a trance.

"Dad!"

He hesitantly replied, "He may be right, Eva."

She turned around and buried her face in her hands again, but this time to hide her anger.

I'm sorry, Eva.

An alert light on the pilots' console suddenly flashed red.

"Satellite feed has detected enemy armor units amassing within the city. They're headed this way," reported Willis.

Gunn looked at Tomo with cold eyes. "Eliminate them."

Tomo nodded, his face expressionless.

Dr. Steiner, his heart heavy, turned to look at his monitor.

Missile turrets protruded from slits in the flesh on Rex-1's back.

"Targets locked," said Tomo.

"Fire!" ordered Gunn.

Instantly, six barrages of Warhawk missiles flew from Rex-1's back like pairs of bullets in one second intervals. They arched up and raced over Moscow. Within ten seconds, they rained down on targets hidden amongst domed buildings. Fire and smoke billowed from each of the six detonations. A few buildings even collapsed like houses of cards.

Gen. Gunn, looking pleased, pointed straight ahead and said, "To the Kremlin."

CHAPTER 6:
BERSERK

Rex-1 took flight. The wind from its wings fanned the flames consuming the base. The Nighthawk followed the cyber-monster to stay in the TP helmet's range. Thousands of Muscovites scurried in panic below them as Rex-1's shadow passed over them. Streets were clogged with traffic. Police car drones scrambled through the crowds trying to maintain a semblance of order. They were failing. Automated firetrucks hurried to burning buildings to snuff the fires, but panicked crowds either hampered them or started more fires. Chaos reigned supreme.

The Kremlin quickly approached.

"Yamamoto, land Rex-1 in Red Square," ordered Gunn.

With a thought, Tomo relayed the commands. Rex-1 swooped down and grinded to a halt, leaving a 50-foot scrape on the Square. The pilots made the Nighthawk circle around the Square, always keeping Rex-1 in view.

Dr. Steiner expelled a long sigh and wiped sweat from his forehead.

The Kremlin seemed empty. Tomo had Rex-1 make an infrared scan of the building. Rainbow-colored blips could be seen throughout it. They were the Coalition's European delegates, all trapped inside. The suddenness of the attack, the panic in the streets, and Rex-1's arrival on the Square likely prevented them from retreating.

"Target acquired," reported Tomo.

Eva never looked up.

"Terminate," commanded Gunn.

Tomo closed his eyes to relay the order.

Rex-1's mouth opened.

BOOM!

A screaming missile exploded against Rex-1's back, pieces of burning skin flying in all directions. The cyborg roared in pain and Tomo cursed in surprise. Everyone grabbed their armrests for dear life. A second missile was blocked when the cyber-dragon's energy shields activated. The pilots started evasive maneuvers as low-flying fighter planes roared over them.

"What was that?" Gunn demanded to know.

"Neo-MIG Shadows," said O'Brian. "They're stealth fighters!"

"I don't care if they're Santa's reindeer! Take them out!" barked Gunn.

"I'm working on it!" shouted Tomo.

The Shadows—all twelve of them—circled around for another strike.

Rex-1's horns glowed, its eyes flared.

The Shadows fired missiles. They all crashed into the cyborg's shields. Cloaked in smoke, Rex-1 roared in defiance and blasted lasers. The Shadows scattered like frightened bees, but not before three exploded.

Rex-1's gaze followed the planes to acquire a new target lock. But without warning, plasma shells buffeted its shield from below. It spun and saw a battle group of Coalition Supertanks emerging from a huge underground bunker near the Kremlin. No doubt it was the leaders' personal defense force. Rex-1 growled as its eyes glowed again and fired. The lasers sliced two tanks in half while the others scattered.

A salvo of missiles exploded on Rex-1's back. It looked over its shoulder and roared at the Shadows, only to be interrupted but a barrage of plasma shells from the Supertanks below. It roared even louder, enraged.

"You're pissing me off!" shouted Tomo. He grimaced as he sent more telepathic commands to Rex-1.

Eva grabbed Dr. Steiner's shoulders. "Dad!"

He turned to her. "What is it?"

"There was a huge spike in autonomous brain activity when Rex-1 was hit by the missiles when its shield was down."

Dr. Steiner's fear melted into confusion. "How's that possible? Our tests said that would be dormant except for essential functions."

This was a bad time for problems. How could they convince Gunn to call off a key mission for a random anomaly? No, it'd have to wait.

They watched as Rex-1 lunged at the Supertanks with a gaping mouth. It clutched one—twice the size of a normal tank—in its jaws. Its teeth dug into the thick titanium armor, crushing it like a can. Rex-1 thrashed it around a few times, then released its grip. The compacted tank flew into a building half-a-mile away. Rex-1 squatted, grabbing another tank with its teeth and clutched one in each hand. It clapped those two like an angry child breaking its toys. Then it tossed what was left of all three on the remaining tanks.

Just then, a red light flashed on Eva's monitor. "Dad! There's another spike! And the shield collapsed!"

There was no time to ask why. Dr. Steiner swiveled his chair to see Gunn. "Get Rex-1 out of there!"

Too late. Before Gunn could argue, they heard Rex-1 bellow in pain on their monitors. They redirected their attentions.

Neo-MIGs flew over Rex-1 as missiles exploded against its back. More skin flew off in flaming clumps. Three surviving Supertanks seized the opportunity, and fired. Plasma shells smashed into the cyborg's chest, ripping into its grafted flesh. Rex-1's eyes and horns glowed as it prepared to retaliate, but it was interrupted by another salvo of missiles fired by the

Shadows. Finally, Rex-1 threw back its head and arms, and bellowed a primal scream.

A warning screen flashed on Eva's computer and a siren-like alarm blared. Her eyes widened in terror. "Readings have spiked through the roof!"

Dr. Steiner jumped to his feet, but before he could yell "Abort," Tomo was screaming.

Lightning-like electricity danced down the wires connecting the TP helmet to the Nighthawk computers. The flyboy's eyes were wide and white, his facial muscles contorted into the face of a terrified banshee as the power surge electrified him. A white aura enveloped him.

"Get the helmet off before it fries his brain!" yelled Dr. Steiner, pointing at Tomo.

Daniels jumped from his chair, fighting turbulence, and grabbed the helmet. Even with gloves on, his hands burned. He grated a cry through his teeth, and ripped the helmet off Tomo's head. They both collapsed on the floor. Smoke emanated from the helmet as it dangled from the wires.

Dr. Steiner immediately looked out the windshield.

More missiles and plasma shells hit Rex-1. Screaming in agony, the cyborg's legs buckled, and it fell against the Kremlin. The building crumbled, burying the cyber-beast under tons of rubble. A thick black cloud of dust flew into the air.

Silence.

Dr. Steiner's jaw dropped. *No! It can't be...*

Suddenly, two red lights flared in the dust cloud, glaring at the Nighthawk. Laser beams fired.

Instantly, the Nighthawk spiraled out of control. The screams of sirens and crewmembers mingled in Dr. Steiner's ears as inertia and vertigo slammed him against the wall. He forced his eyes open and watched through the windshield as the Moscow streets rushed up to them. There was an ear-shattering crash.

Everything went black.

CHAPTER 7:
STRANDED

"Doctor!"

The voice was muffled and distant, like it was coming from the end of a long tunnel.

"Doctor!"

It was louder this time, and closer. Dr. Steiner slowly opened his heavy eyelids. Then he realized his whole body felt heavy. Sparks flashed in his blurry vision, singeing his face. He blinked in desperation. *Focus! Clear up!* The smell of jet fuel hit his nostrils. It only made his heart quicken. He tried to move, but something was pinning him on his back. He couldn't even raise his hands to rub his stinging eyes. He blinked a few more times and the blobs of dark light began to coalesce.

"Doctor!"

"Over here, general!"

Gunn rushed toward Dr. Steiner's voice. In a few seconds, the general was standing over him. His uniform was tattered and torn. His face was cut and bruised. Blood trickled from a huge gash in his forehead.

"Thank God I found you," he said.

"You sound like Daniels," replied Dr. Steiner, trying to smile.

Gunn didn't hear him. He just slipped his hands under the big piece of metal pinning the doctor. Grimacing, he heaved the debris to the side.

"Can you walk?"

Dr. Steiner sat up. "I think so." He slowly stood, using the nearby debris to as a crutch. His legs were stiffer than corpses. He groaned as they took several seconds to get used to his movement and weight. His right cheek felt warm, so his hand reflexively touched it. It was bleeding.

"We can't stay," said Gunn. "The Nighthawk's fuel is leaking and may ignite."

The general about-faced and motioned for Dr. Steiner to follow him. Confused, Dr. Steiner obeyed. They headed for a door leading to a street. Glass and metal crunched under their boots as they jogged toward it. Dr. Steiner glanced back to see a wrecked black hulk with its cockpit ripped open and a scorched broken wing. The entire wall behind it had collapsed. Had they crashed through it?

The two men exited the door, but Gunn didn't stop. He dashed across the debris-littered street. Dr. Steiner barely had time to look around and see wrecked or burning cars a block down each side of the street and the shattered windows on the building they were running toward. A sign written in Russian was prominently displayed above the building's entrance. Dr. Steiner had no idea what it said.

Gunn stopped to open the door and let Dr. Steiner enter first. The doctor slowed his stride as he entered. The room looked like a hotel lobby, and judging by the fresh skid marks on the old linoleum floor, it had been abandoned quickly and recently. A custodian's closet on the far wall was open a crack. Televisions at least fifty years old were still playing Coalition news reports on the attack in several languages. None of that concerned him once he saw the clerk's desk. There stood Tomo, Daniels, and his daughter.

"Eva!"

He rushed toward her and embraced her. She sobbed. He looked at her and brushed her now dirty golden bangs aside so he could see her ocean-blue eyes. Dirt and grime stained her beautiful face. Dr. Steiner put his hands on her tear-smeared cheeks. She looked like the little girl who was scared to see his lab.

"Don't I get a hug, too?" asked Tomo sarcastically.

Dr. Steiner looked over Eva's shoulder to see the young man, who had bruises and small wounds on his face. His black hair was undoubtedly singed, though it was hard to see. His flightsuit was torn, exposing his left shoulder. Blood was seeping between his fingers as he pressed it with his right hand. He was trying hard to grin in spite of it.

Next to him was Daniels. He was leaning on the desk to keep his weight off his right foot. His ankle was probably sprained, if not broken. His trembling hands were burned from saving Tomo. His face seemed uninjured, but his expression was that of a frightened madman. His breathing was quick and erratic, to the verge of hyperventilation. He looked at Dr. Steiner, yet his mind seemed to be somewhere else.

Dr. Steiner sensed Gunn coming up behind him. "Where are Willis and O'Brian?"

"Dead," replied Gunn. "They took the brunt of the crash."

Eva's face suddenly contorted and hardened. She pushed her father out of the way and slapped Gunn. "It's your fault! Your mad thirst for vengeance got us here!"

She tried to slap him again, but Dr. Steiner held her back. She struggled to break free, but quickly tired as tears streaked down her cheeks.

"This is no time for placing blame!" exclaimed Dr. Steiner, releasing Eva.

"Your father's right," said Gunn, hanging his head.

"I just wanna know what the hell happened back there," said Tomo, putting his hands on Eva's shoulders. She quickly brushed them off, saying, "Not now, flyboy!"

"Calm down!" ordered Dr. Steiner.

He sighed, rubbing his eyes, grabbing at scattered thoughts. *Think, Kiefer, think!*

"During the last attack, Eva saw spikes in Rex-1's autonomous brain activity," he began. "That's the amount of operations it performs without commands from Tomo. It's mostly unconscious things like regulating computer systems, just like a human brain maintains a constant heartbeat without any conscious commands. But when Tomo had Rex-1 attack the Coalition forces with tooth and claw, the autonomous activity jumped…my god!"

He paused, his eyes widening.

"What?" injected Tomo.

"The primal attack, the hits from the missiles and shells…they made Rex-1's natural instincts resurface! It thought it was a Tyrannosaurus on the hunt. But when it realized it was in a strange body in a strange place and under attack, it—"

"Went berserk?" interrupted Tomo.

"Essentially, yes," continued Dr. Steiner. "And it broke free of all the fail-safes we put in its systems. That's what caused the power surge that nearly killed you. You're lucky to be alive."

"Ya think?" retorted Tomo, not trying to be funny.

"And then in the chaos, it lashed out and shot us down," said Gunn.

Eva choked back tears and pointed an accusative finger at Gunn. "If you'd just asked for a surrender after destroying the base, this wouldn't have happened."

"We couldn't have known, Eva," said Dr. Steiner. "We never tested Rex-1—"

"Do not call it by that name anymore," interrupted Daniels.

Everyone looked at him.

His timid voice almost boomed. His eyes were bright as fire and cold as death. "It is Apollyon, the Destroyer, the king of the Pit prophesied to rise and smite mankind for its countless millennia of sin. By playing God, you have unleashed His wrath upon the whole of humanity! Now, we will be punished for our arrogance, for spitting in the face of an angry God. What you have unleashed, you cannot stop." His gaze bored into them. "Pray your soul's torment does not continue in an eternity in Hell!"

"Enough of this!" exclaimed Eva, wandering toward the custodial closet. "We need to figure out how we're going to—"

Suddenly, the door behind her flew open and a powerful arm wrapped itself around her neck and pressed knife against her throat.

CHAPTER 8:
THE ENEMY OF MY ENEMY

Eva gasped as the blade cut the surface of her skin. Dr. Steiner felt adrenaline flood his veins, tensing his tired muscles as an ocean of sweat covered his face. Tomo snapped to a karate stance. Gunn clenched his fists. Daniels only hobbled behind the desk to hide.

The arm and knife belonged to a Coalition soldier with shoulders nearly five inches wider than Eva's. His gray uniform indicated he was a grunt, most likely a tank driver. He contorted his stern, bear-like face in anger. His dark eyes burned with hatred, desperation, and confusion.

Dr. Steiner held his hands out to show he was unarmed. "I'm sorry, please—"

The soldier barked at him in a foreign language. Dr. Steiner recognized it immediately.

"He's peaking Russian," he said. "I can't understand him."

"I can," replied Gunn.

Dr. Steiner glanced at the general. "You speak Russian?"

"A little."

"What's he saying?"

Gunn thought for a second, then replied, "He thinks we're am Alliance task force sent to kill any survivors from the attack."

"Your uniforms aren't going to help convince him we're not."

"Don't remind me."

"Tell him we're stranded here just like him."

Gunn sighed. "Give me a second. I haven't spoken this language in over ten years."

The soldier tightened his grip on Eva. A trickle of blood flowed down her neck as the knife cut deeper.

"Talk faster, Gunn!" Dr. Steiner spat. He looked at Tomo. "Calm down so he doesn't think you'll jump him."

Tomo reluctantly lowered his fists.

Gunn rattled off a few sentences of pidgin Russian.

The soldier barked back even louder.

"He doesn't believe me," said Gunn. "He thinks we're controlling the monster and hunting down all his comrades with it."

"Not anymore," injected Tomo.

"*Halt den Mund!*" Dr. Steiner whispered loudly. Tomo got the message.

Eva's terrified eyes pleaded with her father to do something.

Dr. Steiner grunted in frustration. *Damnit! What's it going to take to convince him?*

31

He looked at Gunn. "Tell him we aren't going to kill him. We need his help to survive."

"What?"

"Just do it!"

Gunn fumbled over his words, finally relaying the message in broken sentences.

The soldier started barking a reply, only to be interrupted by Tomo screaming.

Dr. Steiner shot the flyboy an angry glare. "What are you doing?" he shouted.

Tomo's hands were covering his face. "My head! It hurts!"

"Stop it! This isn't helping!"

Tomo didn't hear him. "The voice, it screams! Angry, confused...hungry."

"What are you—"

The ground shook under their feet, but it wasn't an earthquake. The debris jumped like frightened bugs, rattling. Lights flickered. They heard a distant thunder, a thunder with a clock-like rhythm—like a giant's footfalls! The ground shook more as it came closer. *CRASH!* A car fell in front of the door outside. More cars flew past the hotel.

A familiar roar reverberated against the buildings.

"Everybody get down!" shouted Dr. Steiner.

Gunn yelled something in Russian, but the solider already understood. He pulled the knife back and covered Eva with his body. Dr. Steiner grabbed Tomo and shoved him behind the desk, where Daniels was crouched in a ball. The flyboy kept grunting and muttering, so Dr. Steiner covered his mouth with his hand. Gunn quickly joined them.

The ground now quaked under the footfalls. They heard metal grind and concrete shatter. Suddenly, the walking thunder hit the ground in front of the hotel. Glass shattered, raining on their heads. The lights were snuffed. A cloud of dust filled their air and saturated their mouths with a chalky taste. Dr. Steiner's heart jumped to his throat. He felt Tomo's beat like a racecar's motor against his ribcage. *Go before it breaks his ribs!* he wanted to yell. He swallowed it.

But then just as quickly as the thunder came, it dissipated. The footfalls disappeared down the street and the rumbling ground slowly stilled.

After a few moments of silence, Dr. Steiner cautiously stood. The room was darker, foggier. The dust made the light from the shattered windows look murky. He stepped out from behind the desk.

Just then, Eva appeared out of the dust and fell into his arms, crying. She muttered muffled words between sobs, gripping her father's shirt like a frightened child. Dr. Steiner just held her tight.

Gunn was the next to stand. "Where's the Russian?"

Dr. Steiner reluctantly released Eva and looked in the direction she ran from. He took few steps, waving his hand to clear the air, and saw the Russian sitting on the ground Indian-style, breathing heavily. Dust collected on his wet brow. He gave Dr. Steiner a fierce look to hide his fear. He said something in an annoyed tone.

Dr. Steiner looked back at Gunn for a translation.

"He says he believes you," said Gunn.

Dr. Steiner couldn't help but shake his head and snicker a little.

Tomo groaned from behind the desk. Dr. Steiner turned to see him rise from behind it. He was massaging his forehead.

"Do you still have a headache?"

Tomo paused for a second, then looked at the doctor, puzzled. "No."

Dr. Steiner stared off into the empty room, deep in thought.

Gunn helped Daniels stand so he could lean against the desk. He then walked over and offered the Russian a hand. The soldier only scowled at him and stood up by himself.

"Doctor, what happened to me?" asked Tomo.

It sounded like a stupid question, even an inappropriate one, at the time. Eva shot Tomo a glare through teary eyes for it.

After a few seconds of silence, Dr. Steiner looked at Tomo and said, "You're still connected to…"—he hesitated to say "Rex-1"— "…the monster."

"*Nani?*" exclaimed Tomo.

"Somehow, the power surge that fried the helmet also bonded your mind with the monster's. You can't control it, but you can hear its thoughts and sense when it's around. But it only works when it's close by, just like with the TP helmet."

"So that thing is still in my head!"

Dr. Steiner nodded.

Tomo slammed his fist on the desk, cursing.

"But we can use that to our advantage," said Gunn. "Yamamoto can help us know when that thing is nearby. We'll need every advantage we can get."

"Advantages for what?" Tomo demanded to know.

"Getting out of Moscow."

"Are you insane?" retorted Tomo. "There's a cyber-beast running loose, and we're stuck in the middle of an unfamiliar enemy city that's become its new stomping grounds. The only one who could tell us which street is Main Street is more likely to slit our throats than tell us. Any military help we could get is either dead or fighting the monster. None of us are in the physical condition to hike through an urban jungle. And you're worried about tactical advantages?"

"I'm your superior officer!" retorted Gunn. "Do not speak to me like that!"

"Screw this!"

They kept arguing.

Eva leaned against the desk and dropped to the floor. Daniels mumbled incoherent Latin. The Russian just sat, scowling.

Dr. Steiner, however, walked to the door unbeknownst to the rest of them. He stepped gingerly on the broken glass as he exited the door.

Debris was strewn throughout the area. Burning, overturned cars blocked the street. Glass covered the sidewalks like clear snow. There were scrape-like holes along every building where the monster—Apollyon—had bumped into them. Giant footprints were pressed into the street. The smell of broken gas mains and gushing sewer water threatened to suffocate him. Worst of all, there wasn't a soul to be seen. Had they all evacuated? Or were they dead? There was no way to tell.

It was a ghost town haunted by a demon.

Dr. Steiner hung his head, sealed his stinging eyes, and stifled his weeping.

What have I done? I wanted to end a war, not commit genocide. Eva's wrong—this is my fault. I built the monster. Without me, it wouldn't even exist. Now this city—the whole world—is suffering for it. Their blood is on my hands. How much more must be spilled before it ends? Even my daughter nearly died because of it! Daniels is right. I deserve damnation.

He raised his head and looked at the destruction as if to brand it upon his psyche. *I must set it right, somehow, some way, for the sake of my soul. But...*

He turned and dashed back through the door. Everyone was still arguing or moping. He stood before all of them, and shouted, "We're going to destroy the monster!"

PART 2
By Natasha Hayden

CHAPTER 9:
THE LADY BABYLON

At first, they all just stared at him. Dr. Steiner felt a little foolish. Of course he was going to destroy the monster. The necessity of that couldn't be clearer. The question was....

Gunn was first to break the silence and speak the obvious. "How?"

"Yeah, how?" repeated Tomo sarcastically. "You gonna ask it to come home nicely? Or, no, wait, all you have to do is tell it to nuke itself to death. Problem is we'd all end up fried, too. But I think we're all forgetting that this CRAZY MACHINE THAT SHOULDN'T BE ABLE TO EVEN THINK IS *THINKING* IT'S SOME PREHISTORIC DINO—umph!" Gunn had punched him in the gut, and Tomo was now doubled over on the floor.

The general calmly walked toward the door where Dr. Steiner stood. He turned to face the group. "We can't afford anymore hysterics. We need to get moving, and we're going to need all our remaining energy to do it. Dr. Steiner, I appreciate your expertise in this area, but come on, doctor, admit it—you have no more idea how to control this thing than I."

Dr. Steiner did not reply. Gunn was right.

The general moved back into the room and whispered some words into the incoherent chaplain's ear. Daniels straightened, looking slightly more focused.

"Up, all of you! Tomo, help Miss Steiner." Tomo put away the comb he'd just retrieved from his pocket, his hand still shaky, and offered an arm to Eva. Gunn spoke a few words in Russian, and the Russian followed them all out the door.

Tiny particles of debris clouded the air, and they tucked their noses under the collars of their shirts as they stumbled onto the street. Even so, the smell of gas and sewage was pervasive. The Russian took off at a run in an opposite direction of the one they'd chosen, and Gunn's cries for him to stop were to no avail.

"Damn Russian!" he cursed under his breath. "Let's move! Faster!" They were practically running down the street now—at least, as much as a person can run up a mountain—zigzagging between smoking, upturned cars and climbing over rubble.

"What's the point?" Tomo muttered to Dr. Steiner. "We don't even know where we're going."

Dr. Steiner didn't hear him, lost as he was in the deepest reaches of his overworked brain.

A strange sound—any sound but that of smoldering fires and ragged breathing was a shock on the still air—came from the distance behind them and caused them to pause.

"Is it coming back?" Eva asked, clinging to Tomo out of necessity but reaching for her father's familiar though frailer arm.

They all looked to Tomo. "I don't think so," he said uncertainly. "I don't feel anything."

"We can't rely on him," Daniels said, speaking for the first time since they'd begun to move. "His link with Apollyon is a danger to us all—if it exists—and if it doesn't, he is a danger to us still, for he can no more warn you than the Russian could, yet you trust in him. You should all trust in God and be wary of the evil among you."

Eva was looking at him as he said this, and when his eyes fell on her, they were cold and haunted. She looked away and shuddered.

Gunn was kneeling. "Quiet." He pressed his ear to the ground. "Tank."

Even as he said the word, the fog of debris parted at the end of the street, and a tank came bearing down on them.

"Run!" ordered Gunn, leaping to his feet.

They didn't need to be told twice. But the tank gained ground, crushing the scrap metal and bouncing easily over the rubble they'd traversed.

"Faster!" Gunn yelled. It was impossible. Their energy was depleted.

Eva stumbled and fell, bringing Tomo down with her. Dr. Steiner suddenly realized Eva was not behind him and turned, some twenty paces ahead, just in time to see the tank headed straight for his beloved daughter. His heart squeezed in his chest, and he grabbed at it, gasping for air.

The tank stopped just short of crushing the two on the ground. The top opened. A familiar face popped up, and then a strong body followed, leaping nimbly down to the ground and offering his support to Eva. It was the Russian.

Dr. Steiner began to breathe again, but he had to sit down while his heart palpitations normalized. Gunn and Daniels soon trotted back from their position at the head of the group and helped Dr. Steiner to his feet. Eva and Tomo were already crawling into the tank.

Dr. Steiner did not ask Gunn if he thought this was a good idea, though he had his doubts, but he already knew what Gunn would say. Indeed, the general had focused his steely gaze on the Russian who waited for him, and as soon as they were near, he began a heated discussion. On Gunn's part, it was partly Russian, partly English, and partly cursing. Dr. Steiner couldn't tell what the Russian said, but the man looked sincere. Whether he was sincerely out to hurt or to save them was yet to be seen.

Dr. Steiner thought he'd take his chances. A tank was much better than running.

"Thank you," he said in English as the Russian helped him climb up. The Russian nodded curtly. Inside the tank, Dr. Steiner spoke quietly to Gunn. "What was all that about?"

"Aren't you at all curious about how our Russian managed to find a working tank, a supposedly empty one at that?" Gunn returned.

"The thought had crossed my mind."

"From what I can make out, he says it was abandoned. Why do you abandon a good tank in the middle of battle? Unthinkable."

Eva was squeezed in by her father and overheard this last comment. "Maybe they saw the monster and ran for cover in a building."

Dr. Steiner nodded.

Gunn glared at them. "Don't you start believing for a minute that this Russian is up to any good."

"He's the first good that's come our way," Dr. Steiner pointed out.

"Hey, does this thing have a radio?" Tomo asked suddenly from the back of the tank.

"Already checked," Gunn said. "Blown out."

"Well, that's unlucky," Tomo said, deflated. "How did that happen?"

"That's what I've been wondering," Gunn said darkly.

Eva wanted to ask where they were going, but she didn't want to give any more fuel to the general's distrust. As far as she was concerned, they all wanted away from the monster, and this was their best bet. In the muted darkness of the tank, a crawling sensation began to creep over her arms and up her neck. She attributed it to nerves, but when she looked up, a pair of gleaming, white eyes were still visible, and they were looking straight at her. Daniels.

In the silence and dark, his voice was that of a ghost. "Behold, the punishment of the great prostitute, who sits on many waters. With her the kings of the earth committed adultery. She sits on the scarlet beast, and on her forehead is written: 'Mystery, Babylon the Great, the Mother of Prostitutes and of the Abominations of the Earth.'"

"Can you get him to *shut up?*" whined Tomo from his corner.

"Gunn, is he stable?" whispered Dr. Steiner. They listened quietly for a minute.

The chaplain's foreboding words had dissolved into Latin supplications.

The hard edge was erased from Gunn's tone when he spoke next. "He's been through a lot in his life. The events of this last year have been very hard on him, and I imagine the trauma of today has pushed him a little over the edge, as it has for all of us. But he's a chaplain, a former monk. He means no harm. He speaks against your creation, Dr. Steiner, and as long as your goal is to destroy it, he is not your enemy."

The way Gunn tried to distance himself from the monster was not lost on Dr. Steiner. "This is not just *my* creation, General Gunn. All of us here have had a part, even our Russian, for without his kind there would have been no need for such an..."—he had been about to say "abomination" but thought better of the word in front of the chaplain—"a weapon," he finished instead. "But I will assume responsibility for its destruction."

"Any progression on that thought?" the general asked testily.

"I'm working on it," the doctor muttered.

A sudden explosion rocked the tank.

"Have we been hit?" Eva screeched.

"Gunn?" Dr. Steiner asked.

The Russian was muttering to himself, and Gunn was listening to him.

"Gunn?" the doctor repeated.

"No, we haven't been hit. There's some fighting going on above us."

"Fighting? Against whom?" Dr. Steiner asked. "Is it our side?"

And that's when they heard Tomo groaning and muttering behind them in the dark.

"Guess who's back," Gunn said, stepping over limbs to reach the console and speak to the Russian.

Eva whimpered.

They listened fearfully for several minutes. Even the Russian and Gunn fell silent. And then they heard it, the awful *THUD* as the giant placed its claws, the screeching and scraping of metal against metal and concrete, the distant explosions of battle. Another closer explosion rocked them again. Eva clutched her father's arm and muffled her scream into it.

The tank stopped.

"Why are we stopping?" asked Dr. Steiner.

Gunn turned to them, his gaze pensive. "The Russian says he saw the direction the monster took as he was looking for a tank, and he adjusted our course accordingly. It's coming back." He looked Dr. Steiner in the eye. "Is there a reason it would do that, doctor?"

Dr. Steiner thought it, and Gunn voiced it. "There should be no reason for the thing to retrace its path. There should be nothing to hold it in place and keep it from wandering the world. It can fly, after all. And if it does possess the mind of an animal, it should be running for safety by now. So, what reason does it have to return to the fight?"

The doctor instinctively looked to Tomo.

"We know they're linked," Gunn said.

"This is all new to me," Dr. Steiner murmured. "I wouldn't have thought any sort of mental link possible, not without the appropriate technology."

"Which we had and lost, and the link's still there, doctor."

"*Jah*, though the science of it baffles me. I'm afraid we can't rule out anything at this point. All evidence affirms the impossible. They are linked, but the question is how much? More than we'd thought, it would appear. The monster won't leave Moscow. It can't leave because Tomo is here."

"So, *why* are we stopped, again?" Eva hissed, her fear clenching her teeth tight.

"We have to get out."

"*What?*"

"You could have mentioned this sooner," Dr. Steiner said, alarmed.

"*Why?*"

"We're in the creature's path," Gunn said, "and according to the Russian, this was the only tank that wasn't cleaved in two."

The Russian had been waiting for them to finish speaking, and now Gunn nodded at him. With a lurch, the tank moved forward and crashed through a brick wall. Glass shattered outside. The *THUDs* were getting much closer.

"I thought we were getting out!" Eva said.

"Now we are," Gunn said, as the Russian opened the top and pushed debris out of the way. "There's a better chance of the tank surviving under cover like this."

They climbed through the opening, and Gunn pulled Tomo through. The flyboy's eyes were glazed.

"I'm not going out on that street," Tomo moaned. "It's looking for me."

The others exchanged glances over his head.

"He can't know that for sure, can he, doctor?"

"I don't know."

"Let's hope there's a back door," Gunn said.

The Russian was already ahead of the game, calling to them from deeper inside the building. They'd landed in an apartment. As they caught up with the Russian, they heard voices and pulled up short. The Russian was talking hurriedly with someone.

Gunn listened and then blew air forcefully through pursed lips. "There are civilians still in this building."

They reached the Russian, and he motioned for them to continue farther. And then he turned and disappeared.

"Where's he going?" Eva shouted, as Gunn, Daniels, and Tomo followed the Russian's directions. Dr. Steiner stood undecided with his daughter.

"Come on!" Gunn shouted back. "Doctor Steiner, bring your daughter. You can't help them. We need you to stop this thing. Let's go!"

Dr. Steiner and Eva stumbled together toward the others, and they raced down the long hall to a door with no markings. When they opened it, an alarm sounded in the building.

"Well, that should help," Dr. Steiner said as they filed quickly outside into a smaller street than the one they'd left. At one end to the north, they could see the smoking remains of the Kremlin, very close now, just across the Moscow River, with a bridge still intact. But they didn't want to be in the center of the city, so they turned the other direction.

Tomo was already staring up with bulging eyes. Daniels clutched his cross above his head, but it was not pointed at the monster, which stood just across the building on the street they'd just left. It had stopped and seemed to be searching.

"Quiet. Steady, now," Gunn said. "Nobody make—"

But he didn't get to finish his sentence. With the screeching pierce of metal grinding against metal, the monster tossed what looked to be a toy in its jaws toward the place where they stood. The aim was off, or it would have killed them all right there. Eva saw enough to see that it was their very own tank that bounced through the back of the apartment building, hit the street, and skidded through the building on the opposite side. And then she flew backward through the air and the wall of dust smothered her.

She woke up, flat on her back, and could see nothing, hear no one, not even the monster. She was choking on dust. Slowly, achingly, she turned to her side and attempted to lift herself from the ground. She had to stop as a fit of coughing weakened her limbs. She lifted her blouse to try to block out some of the dust. Her eyes were full of grit, but she fought to keep them open. She couldn't call out. Every time she opened her mouth, she choked, so she tried breathing through clenched teeth. She peered into the murky light around her, and then she saw a figure moving toward her. She sighed in relief and waved so he would see that she was alive.

The figure was nearly on top of her before she realized who he was. She had seen the cross and known where it was pointed before the tank had come crashing down. And she knew she was not rescued, after all, as the cross came down across her vision and sent her reeling into oblivion with its blow.

***

The Russian slowly awoke from unconsciousness, his last memory being of a horrible crashing noise that had suddenly ripped the room in which he'd been standing in two. He tried to move his legs, but he could barely feel them. He opened his eyes and sucked in a great breath at once and then wished he hadn't as the dust rolled in. When the choking had subsided, he tried again, more carefully. Since his lower body didn't seem to be working, he twisted his head to try to get his bearings. The first thing he noticed was the pile of broken wall at his feet and partially covering him. So, that's why he couldn't move his legs. The second thing he realized was that he was in an open area, which meant he was no longer on the second story of the building. He'd fallen to the street below. It was a wonder he wasn't dead.

He twisted his neck back, trying to peer behind his head, and movement caught the corner of his eye. As he watched, a large, bulky figure staggered out of the swirling fog just a few paces away. The shape was odd, and it took him a moment to realize that it wasn't just one large person but two small ones, the second thrown over the first's shoulder.

He tried to speak, to call out, but his voice came out as little more than a gasp. Nonetheless, the figure turned toward the sound. The Russian found he could move his arm, and he reached out weakly. The figure hesitated, then took a tentative step toward him. The Russian called out again and managed to whisper a Russian plea for help. The figure abruptly stopped and then turned away, picking up his lopsided pace, but the Russian had seen. The burning eyes behind broken and smudged spectacles that had pierced him through the mist could belong to only one man. It was the American priest, the one they called Daniels. The Russian was Greek Orthodox by faith, and so at first, he had respected the sign of the cross around the priest's neck and what it represented. But the longer he'd spent in the company of the man, the more unnerved he'd become. The Russian was not a superstitious man, but when he looked into the eyes of the priest, he felt an emptiness and a darkness that made the hair on his arms stand on end.

But it was not these thoughts alone that assailed him in the few seconds he watched until the priest disappeared. The figure draped over the priest's shoulder frightened him more. That long blond hair could belong to only one person, the beautiful woman they called Eva, and it was immediately clear to the Russian's mind that whatever the priest was doing with her, he was up to no good.

The priest had disappeared by now, but the Russian knew he had to go after him. Fresh adrenaline pounded through his veins, and with all the remaining strength he could muster, he pushed at the layers of brick that covered his body. Pulling and scraping, he managed to free his legs one by one, and then he stood shakily to his feet and lurched painfully into the fog.

With zealous fervor in his heart, Daniels shouldered his burden and plodded forward with more strength than his gaunt figure and sprained ankle should have allowed. He knew his destination wasn't far, maybe a kilometer, certainly less than a mile. Though Eva was slight, she still should have been a heavy burden for even such a meager distance, but

Daniels was on a mission of end-of-the-world proportions, and no pain could even tempt him to stop for a rest. He felt certain no one could have followed him. He'd seen Gunn out cold, had even checked to make sure his old friend was breathing, and there was no way the Russian—may God rest his ungodly soul in damnation—could have freed himself from the building's rubble.

The wide streets around the Kremlin should have been filled with moving traffic but, instead, were filled with ghost vehicles. There was an unearthly stillness on this day of defeat and Almighty judgment. The air was clearer here near the river that lay to his right. The Kremlin continued to burn on his left. He turned into Red Square and saw it across the vast expanse, now decorated with a new fifty-foot gash and burning debris, St. Basil's Cathedral. Miraculously, it still stood, though perhaps two or three onion domes short. It was a sign of God. The seat of heathen power lay demolished and smoking just two stones' throws away, but the House of God still stood strong.

He approached it more quickly now, new strength flowing through his extremities—a blessing of God and a sign of His favor, most assuredly—and climbed the steps to enter the dim, holy light of the church's sanctuaries.

It was here that he would purify the demons from this woman of science—this adulteress woman of Babylon who did not believe in the Almighty—and if he was not successful, he would leave her to be destroyed by the evil that was of her own making. It was a just end.

Gunn had rounded up Dr. Steiner and Tomo, amazingly relatively unscathed though they'd all been knocked unconscious, and now they were scouring the street and calling out for Eva and Daniels, who were nowhere to be found.

"Doctor, we must go. We're wasting time," Gunn said, his tone tinged with true regret.

"She's my daughter!" Dr. Steiner shouted. "Eva! EVA!" He wandered into the middle of the street and stood there, looking like the lost man he was.

Gunn approached him quietly and put a gentle hand on his shoulder. "I've lost a friend, too, but doctor, how many more will die if we can't complete our mission?"

"I haven't lost her! You don't know that, not yet!" Dr. Steiner cried. But at the same time, he knew the truth of the general's words, and after a few silent moments, he turned to face him, eyes lifeless. "We'll come back," he said, but he looked as if he didn't believe it. The three of them walked down the street like a three-legged horse, their arms around each other in support.

The Russian finally came into clearer air, his eyes scanning the distance. Yes, there. A figure strode with unwavering purpose down the street, around the Kremlin. The Russian knew then where he was headed and tried to speed up his own labored limp. He was bleeding into his boots. He could feel the blood pooling and squishing with every step. He refused to look down and survey the damage. The woman was in danger, and he had somehow become linked to her fate. That bond had formed, even as his knife had pressed against her throat. He couldn't say what had possessed him to grab her like that, but he believed in Providence. And for the pain he'd caused her, he would now atone.

These thoughts occupied his mind, but as it had for Daniels, the emptiness of this once great city crept upon his mind. Even ten years ago, his beloved Moscow had been full of life, full of a variety of cultures and old and new Russian history blending into one beautiful tapestry. But in the last few years, the years of war, this powerful city had faded to a mere husk of its former glory. The streets which had been so crowded before slowly began to empty as their visitors and then their citizens began to migrate to other safer, less central, war zones—for there was no place now that wasn't a war zone. Gorky Park, Arbat Street, once so full of happy strollers and shoppers, had become places where people walked quickly, speaking to no one, not daring to show life and single themselves out. And then Moscow had barricaded itself in. Those who remained hadn't gotten out in time. That was why the city was so empty now.

At first, when the dragon had flown over the city, it had caused a panic, filling the streets once more as families ran to find each other, but Muscovites knew what to do when there was trouble—run and hide. They had learned already in this war that there was no escape, and they would remain and die in their homes...like those he'd discovered in the apartment.

He forcefully pushed these thoughts away as he turned the corner and his suspicions about Daniels' destination were confirmed. There was one life, at least, whose outcome he could change, if he was not already too late. He cursed his un-cooperating limbs.

Eva woke to a nightmare. She was drowning! She searched for the surface, tried to suck in air and found only water. She coughed and heaved but couldn't move. She was trapped, tied down in the water! She didn't have a chance. As her lungs filled, she began to black out again.

The flow of water abruptly stopped. Hands pumped her stomach. Air was forced through her lungs. She heaved the water out of her and opened her eyes.

The nightmare wasn't over. Dirty, broken spectacles hovered above her. A thin, rough and burned hand lightly slapped her face, trying to rouse her. Daniels. Frantically, she tried to sit up, and when that failed, she twisted her head back and forth, attempting to see where she was.

Very dim light filtered through small windows. The walls around her rose into a distant dome above her head. Her wrists and ankles were tied down on some sort of table, and a basin of water sat at her feet. The clouds in her mind suddenly scattered, and she knew what sort of place she was in, if not exactly where. This was a church, and she was lying on an altar...and a basin of holy water had just been dumped down her throat. It would have been comical, if she had not been so terrified.

Eva met the dark eyes of the chaplain.

"You will thank me when I have purified your soul," he said.

Eva stared at him in disbelief. "When *what*? You've gone mad!"

The chaplain stood straight. "The demons of lust and hatred still inhabit your being. You should have let the holy water cleanse you. Where water did not work, perhaps fire will." He turned away.

"*What*?" Eva repeated. She lifted her head and pulled at her bonds, both desperate to escape and to see what was coming next. "Wait! You can't do this! My father is working to save us. Why are you doing this? What have *I* done?"

Daniels turned back to her, his hands still empty for now. "You know your part full well, harlot," he said calmly. "You have seduced our minds. You are wicked. These are your sins. Know yourself so that you can be healed: you put your adulterous mind to the task of creating a creature of Hell. You will not admit your guilt, even dishonoring your father by your faithlessness. You are a distraction and a seduction to Tomo, and you confuse him when he should be focused on the task of undoing your evil. You have broken the commandments in full: you have created an idol and worshiped its power; you have murdered, dishonored your father, lied, cursed, coveted, stolen, and committed adultery. What you have done in the secret places of your mind will now be revealed to all, for even the thought of these deeds is as wicked as the act."

"How can you say that?" Eva asked, her voice reaching hysteria. "How am I more guilty than you? From the *beginning*, I didn't believe this was right!"

"Yet you did not stop it."

"And so it's all *my* fault now? You know nothing about me—not my thoughts or what I've done! Please, just let me go! This is not helping anything."

"God has turned against us because of you. I must obey him first." The chaplain turned away from her quickly now, and when he whirled about to face her again, he held a long, unlit, oil-burning candle in his hands. As she watched, too horrified to make a sound, he poured the oil out over her blouse in the symbol of a cross. Then she began to scream.

The Russian felt faint when he reached the door of the cathedral. He didn't pause to rest, afraid of what might be happening inside. He squished down the dim hallways with each step, looking through doorways, listening for any sound out of the ordinary. And then he heard the screaming.

Tomo had learned to recognize the early warning signs that the beast was near. It began as a soft buzz at the base of his skull, and then his vision began to go slightly blurry as that other consciousness layered itself over his own. He stopped, halting his companions, and waited for the thunderous sounds of movement which would signal the monster's direction of approach.

There weren't any.

"Where is it?" he cried as the pain increased.

Gunn and Dr. Steiner exchanged a look.

"The artillery's been slowing down," Gunn said. "Either the machine has gotten away, or...or they're running out of ammunition."

They looked at Tomo again. He was bent double, hands over his head, shielding himself from the approach that didn't seem to be coming.

"It's not gone," Dr. Steiner said. And then a strange metallic beat sounded over their heads, and a stream of fire exploded over the building they were sheltered against. They stared up at the plated belly, intermittent tatters of grafted skin trailing underneath, that flew above them. A lone missile whistled toward the beast, missed, and exploded somewhere over residential Moscow. The beast seemed to hesitate in the air. Tomo didn't appear to be breathing. Dr. Steiner crouched near the ground, staring up at this impossible invention he had created to be indestructible and which he now had to destroy.

The beast did not land. After a moment, it flew on back the way they had just come from, toward the center of Moscow. Dr. Steiner prayed his daughter was safe or already dead, someplace where she wouldn't be able to feel pain.

***

"No!" the Russian bellowed in his native tongue, stumbling into the chapel just in time to see Daniels lowering a small flame toward a screaming Eva. He didn't know what the priest had already done to her, but the sight of her there, helpless, spurred on whatever adrenaline he had left. It was barely enough to help him walk straight. He thought he was rushing toward her, and in his mind, he was, but in reality, he was stumbling unsteadily and making little headway.

49

Daniels looked up at his cry, the candle hovering dangerously close to Eva's heaving chest. He should have killed the infidel when he had the chance, was the chaplain's immediate thought. Then he saw the man's pathetic attempts to reach the altar, and he began to laugh, a sound that reverberated eerily under the dome.

Eva ceased her screaming as she heard the laugh. The face above her tilted to the ceiling, unheeding of the wax that sloshed down the candle's side, spilling onto his already charred and numb hand. For a moment, she forced her gaze from the dripping wax and the sputtering flame and turned her pleading eyes toward the Russian. If his own adrenaline had failed him, those eyes aroused new strength in his limbs, and he labored more steadily toward her.

The building shook, and a tremendous metallic roar echoed under the domes of the cathedral. Daniels' laugh turned maniacal, and he lifted his face and hands to the sky as the dome above them was ripped away by a heavy, plated tail.

He screamed his words toward heaven: "Behold! The punishment of the great prostitute, who sits on many waters! She who rules over the kings of the earth will meet her ruin on the very beast she rides! And the beast will hate the prostitute and will eat her flesh and burn her with fire. And God will give the power to the beast until his words are fulfilled!"

As he spoke, large drops of wax splashed free of their bonds and rained fire onto Eva's exposed limbs. She screamed, a sound that curled the Russian's toes and sent a tingle all the way up his spine and into his skull, and then, as if to vindicate the ranting of a madman, a hot blast of flame and a thunderous metallic crash brought the last of St. Basil's Cathedral raining down on their heads. As the world-known face of the once beautiful Moscow fell, the Russian knew that neither would rise from these ashes. He had no time to mourn.

Heavy shards struck the three of them, but a particularly large chunk of concrete made a direct hit on the priest's head, and he fell. The Russian did not look to see his fate. He fought as though swimming upstream until he reached the woman on the altar. He beat out the flames that had begun to consume her blouse, and he cut her bonds quickly with his knife. She was unconscious as he shoved her into an alcove and covered her body with his own.

CHAPTER 10:
THE ENEMY OF MY ENEMY
(PART 2)

Dr. Steiner had no time to consider what new havoc the monster was wreaking now that it had taken to the air. The onslaught of artillery had kept it bound to the ground before, but no longer.

"I need to get an aerial view of that thing," Dr. Steiner told Gunn as they helped a shaky Tomo to his feet. Tomo was getting accustomed to this by now, and he was quicker to recover.

"Are you crazy?" the flyboy stated, gasping for breath. He hadn't been breathing as the monster had passed, after all.

"I need to examine its path," Dr. Steiner clarified.

"How the hell do you think you're going to do *that*?" Tomo yelled. "Get up there and fly around with your old chum, the BEASTIE?"

Gunn laid a restraining hand on Tomo's shoulder. "I realize you're shaken up, son, and I understand, but I think Doctor Steiner may be right. We're stuck if we don't get some sort of advantage over this thing."

"This *thing*, this THING! Do you hear yourselves? There *is* no advantage when you can't even identify something *you* created!"

"But I *did* create it," Dr. Steiner said softly. "I know it better than anyone, except maybe...." He didn't finish that thought as a choking grief reared up, and Gunn put a reassuring hand on his shoulder, too. "If anyone has a chance here, we do," Dr. Steiner finally finished.

"Which is why we need to find some sort of headquarters and get some help," Gunn said firmly, taking control. "Let's move while we're still able."

"What exactly do you mean by 'headquarters'?" Tomo asked warily as they stumbled down the street once more.

"Trust me."

"A military base?" Dr. Steiner asked.

Gunn nodded grimly.

"Where are we going to find a friendly...?" Tomo began. "Oh...you *can't* be serious!"

"Dead serious."

"You've got to be kidding me."

It didn't take long. Gunn directed them toward the last sounds of gunfire they'd heard. As they approached the area, the sounds of shouting voices and scrambling boots guided them further. The street they turned onto contained a new level of rubble and flying dust they had not yet seen. The sun was nowhere to be found beneath the dirty clouds.

It took some time for them to be noticed, and it was a sign of the enemy's dwindling confidence and resources that they weren't shot on sight. They were soon surrounded by ten armed men, none unscathed, who yelled at them in Russian until they were face down on the ground, fingers interlocked behind their heads.

Finally, the soldiers quieted down enough that Gunn was able to understand a question directed at the three of them. He raised one hand above his head and lifted his eyes, and when no one stopped him, he spoke loudly.

"We can help you!" he said in the Russian he knew. "We know how to stop the machine. We just need your help!"

The Russians quickly deliberated among themselves, and then in a flash, they were pulling Gunn to his knees by the hair and yelling at him as he yelled back. Tomo and Dr. Steiner remained helplessly on the ground as cold rifles nudged the backs of their heads.

Suddenly, the yelling match was over, and the Russians shoved Gunn roughly toward his friends. He caught himself on all fours. The guards standing over the other two lifted their rifles and stepped away.

Dr. Steiner looked up cautiously and then unlaced his fingers slowly. He glanced toward Gunn. "What's going on?"

"May I translate?" Gunn asked their captors in Russian. The soldiers were deliberating again, and finally, they grabbed Tomo off the ground and began to drag him off.

"Hey! What's happening? What are you doing to me? Hey, what are they doing to me?" he yelled as they kept dragging him down the street away from his companions. His terrified yells were silenced after they could no longer see him, and Dr. Steiner looked at Gunn, wide-eyed. A soldier barked at Gunn, and the general turned to the doctor and spoke slowly and calmly.

"They don't want the three of us to conspire together. I told them you were the one who knew how to stop the machine, and they agreed to let me translate for you."

"But I *don't* know how to stop the machine," whispered Dr. Steiner.

"Then I suggest you figure that out." Gunn nodded to the soldiers.

"Will I have access to what I need?" Steiner asked as the soldiers nudged them to their feet.

"They're taking us to the base now."

The arduous pace the soldiers pushed, and the maze of debris, kept them from talking more. They trekked down the long street, which opened into a slightly wider one. A short way down this second, the soldiers turned toward a building that was still half intact. They spoke quickly with the guard at the entrance and then continued down a hallway, stooping along much of it. The building appeared to have been a government office before the attack. At another door, they talked to the guards, one of whom opened the door and ran ahead of them down a set of steep stairs. They entered a basement, which appeared to be in better shape than it should have been given the upheaval upstairs, and finally, they came to a more official-looking door. This one had heavy metallic plating and guns protruding from the wall on either side. Only two guards stood here, but they were fully loaded with artillery.

The soldier who'd run ahead must have prepared the way because the guards stepped aside, and the door swished open, retracting into the wall to let them through and then sealing them in again on the other side. They passed through a long, dimly lit and heavily fortified passage that ended in a set of stairs leading farther underground.

Eventually, they emerged into another hallway and finally found themselves being led by a close press of guards into a war room complete with satellite screens, maps, communications systems, and all sorts of army headquarters paraphernalia. Gunn noticed immediately that many of the screens were dark or a static white.

"Do you think we can have a go at those radios?" Dr. Steiner asked.

"I doubt it. They'll be keeping a close eye on us here. One misstep, and we're goners. What do you need?"

The Russians eyed them warily, and Gunn had a quick exchange with a soldier who then relayed a message to the Russian Commander across the room. Apparently, they were to communicate only in this childish game of "telephone" with the man in charge. Dr. Steiner just hoped their lines wouldn't get crossed in the red tape of politics. He had work to do, and he didn't need anything that would slow him down. But he had to admit, this location was much better than he could have hoped for his work, and he wouldn't complain about the methods as long as he could get the Russians to agree to give him what he needed. He relayed his requests to Gunn and settled in for the wait.

Eva awoke disoriented. At first, she thought she was still on the altar and that Daniels had fallen on top of her. But she was on her side, and her wrists were free. She could see them in front of her face. She struggled to move, twisting her arms around to push at the warm body on top of her, but it was too heavy, dead weight. Then she felt the wetness pooled under her calves.

Am I bleeding? she thought. *I'm bleeding and pinned under a dead man! I'm going to die.* Somehow, that thought brought her peace. If she was going to die, at least she'd been given the gift of knowing beforehand. There were issues she had to resolve in her heart. Crazy Daniels had been right about some things. She knew that to commit the sins he'd listed, even if just in her heart, was to commit the sins, period. She'd heard that in Sunday School so long ago, when her mother had still been alive. Eva had grown up to be a woman of science. She had still believed in God somewhere deep in the recesses of her soul, but she had been following her own way for a long time.

It had been wrong to create the death machine; she'd been right to oppose it. That was the wrong use for her knowledge of science. But she had helped create it, nonetheless, and in her heart she'd put all the blame on her father. And if he was still alive, he carried that blame now, all by himself, all alone. The thought made her weep. She might never live to tell him she was sorry. It might be too late already.

Her body heaved with sobs so that it was some time before she realized that something was stroking her hair, whispering to her. Not some*thing*. Some*one*.

"D-Daniels?" She wasn't sure she wanted to know the answer. She didn't want that sick man near her ever again, especially not stroking her hair.

"Sasha," the voice said, and she sighed in relief, hearing the Russian speak his name.

He shifted his weight off her, and she could finally see better. They were in a recess in the wall, surrounded by large chunks of wall and ceiling. The cathedral was destroyed. Where the altar had once been, there was a large pile of rubble. No sign of Daniels. She began to cry again. She would be dead were it not for the kindness of this stranger, a man who had once put a knife to her throat. She knew he meant her no harm now. She didn't know how, but he had found her and saved her from the madman. She trusted him fully.

The Russian pulled himself to a sitting position and put her head in his lap, stroking her hair as she continued to cry, the tenseness caused by her ordeal finally releasing itself. Eventually, she remembered the blood, and she sat up. The effort caused her to flinch in pain. The Russian—Sasha— spoke softly to her and put a restraining hand on her shoulder, but she struggled against it. Her skin burned, and she looked down at the exposed flesh of her arms and stomach. Her blouse was ripped and charred. Where her blouse had burnt away completely, there were dark burns that ached with every movement. Dried wax clung to her arms, and she could feel the burns there, too. But the blood. Where was the blood from?

Then she saw it. It covered her legs, but it wasn't hers. She couldn't look at the deep gashes any longer, so she turned her gaze to her rescuer's face, eyes wide and frightened.

He shook his head, as though to say it was no matter. He took off his light military jacket, so that he wore only a tank top over taut chest muscles, and put the garment carefully over her shoulders. He pointed to the wounds on her belly, concern in his eyes.

"I'm okay," she said gratefully, tears welling up in her eyes again. "Thank you." The Russian understood these last words and smiled, his hand reaching for her hair again. She couldn't say why she wanted, needed, that touch so much, but she leaned into it and closed her eyes. The Russian pulled her against his chest, humming a lullaby of a tune in a sweet tenor until they both drifted to sleep.

Dr. Steiner was finally looking at proof of what he'd guessed all along, impossible as it was.

"See here," he said to Gunn, pointing at the satellite read-out they'd obtained. They'd been fortunate to get it. The monster had inadvertently destroyed much of their satellite connection. Steiner drew a circle with his fingers over the map they were looking at. "Five miles. Five miles in every direction from these points remains untouched. It's going in circles. I'm not sure it can leave."

"Why would that be?" Gunn asked. Some of the soldiers, though they had been giving them plenty of room to work, now leaned in close to study the maps, too. Even the Commander stood up across the room, curious as to what the interest was. He sent a man scurrying over to find out for him.

"See this line in the middle?"

Gunn nodded.

"This is *our* path. This is where we fell, and this is where we are now."

"It's following us?"

"In a manner of speaking. Really, it can't leave."

"It has wings. It could be halfway to China by now!"

"It *won't* leave, I mean. Not while it's connected to Tomo."

"That's preposterous!"

The soldiers were now looking at each other uneasily, gripping their guns a little tighter. The messenger spoke quickly to Gunn, but Gunn ignored him.

"You want me to tell the Commander over there that our man is controlling the monster? If they don't laugh at us, they'll shoot us! Either way, so much for our free pass to the war room. We'll be out of the job before we've even started! And you can die with the knowledge that you singlehandedly unleashed the Apocalypse on the world!"

Dr. Steiner turned to face Gunn, ignoring the growing agitation of the soldiers and the demands of the Commander's messenger. His voice was even-tempered, but his words were firm, unyielding.

"If the Apocalypse has been unleashed on the world, it didn't start today, and it wasn't by the efforts of one man alone. All the world is guilty. My friend, you should look to your own conscience and not be so worried about that of others. Now, if you would please tell the Commander's messenger that I am fairly certain the monster won't leave Moscow, I think we can leave him to his own devices about the reason.

"You're right; it wouldn't be prudent to tell him why. They would probably kill Tomo, and if they do that, there's no telling where the monster will go. Best to keep it close for now. If he presses us, tell him I'm working on the hows and whys, and I am. I need to figure out a way we can use this to our advantage. Meanwhile, get me a large sheet of paper. I want to make a diagram of Rex-1 from memory."

Dr. Steiner stared at his diagram and then closed his eyes tightly, trying to remember if there was anything missing. He'd labeled everything, and Gunn was staring over his shoulder, reading.

"What about there?" Gunn pointed to a spot on the diagram.

"That's empty space. It was for a nuclear warhead, but I pulled it from the project. Frankly, why risk a nuke and all that radiation when we have a fire-breathing, laser-shooting dragon in the air, huh?" The situation was too serious to even smile.

Dr. Steiner closed his eyes and concentrated again, but Gunn cleared his throat meaningfully. "I have a confession to make," Gunn said.

Dr. Steiner opened his eyes. "What is it?"

"That space may not be empty space, after all."

"What do you mean?" The doctor's words were tense now.

"We may have used that space, is all I'm saying. *I'm* the general, in case you forgot. It was *my* call to make, not yours."

"What did you *do?*" Dr. Steiner asked, beginning to feel ill. "Did you add the nuke?"

Gunn suddenly stood tall, and his voice became steely. "If you had done your job correctly, the use of that nuke would be entirely in *my* capable hands. Besides, the objective here was to destroy the enemy, and I'm starting to wonder, doctor, how loyal you actually are to that objective. Don't you forget that it was one of these soldiers who held a knife to your daughter's throat. Is that the kind of man you want to let live?"

This reminder of his daughter's plight broke Dr. Steiner. He turned away, his pain evident on his face. "Still, it isn't my place to destroy anyone, and had I been listening to my daughter in the first place, she wouldn't have ended up here. If my objective was to destroy these men, I was wrong. My objectives have changed now, general, and there's only one thing I want destroyed, if *you* haven't reached our hand so far forward that we can't draw it back."

"Fool!" Gunn said quietly. "We can use that weapon to destroy the thing! We just need a way to get to it."

"If that nuke goes off, Moscow goes, too."

"I know," the general said coldly.

"I can't let that happen. There are innocent people here. You saw them. We need to think of another way."

"If we don't destroy Moscow and all evidence of what happened here, the Coalition will sting us back like an angry hive of bees."

"We've already broken their power in half," Steiner pointed out.

Gunn ignored him. "If you can *get* to that bomb, you tell me."

Dr. Steiner turned away, muttering to himself.

"*What* was that, doctor?"

"I don't think it's possible anyway, not without a controller. We're at the mercy of that beast, if it should figure out how to let the bomb go by itself. Obviously, it hasn't yet."

"We *have* a controller."

"Tomo can't control that thing. He's *connected* to it, not in control of it."

"We don't know *what* he can do," Gunn said darkly. "We need to try."

"No, no, NO!" Dr. Steiner said, but Gunn was already speaking to the Commander's messenger.

"You can't bring Tomo into this," Dr. Steiner pleaded. "I thought we'd decided that!"

"Are you going to do your job, doctor, or should I tell them you're of no further use?" Gunn threatened. "They won't kill Tomo if they think he's their only chance. They won't see what hit them."

Gunn grinned darkly, and at that moment, Dr. Steiner knew he was on his own. He would have to figure out a way to kill the monster *and* save Moscow from utter destruction, all under Gunn's nose and with his help but without the man guessing that his plan wasn't the one in play.

CHAPTER 11:
DO OR DIE

Dr. Steiner knew he didn't have much time. Whatever Gunn was planning, he was working quickly, concocting some sort of story for the Russians, and Steiner wondered if it wouldn't have been better to play along for awhile, because now Gunn wasn't telling him anything. The one good thing to come out of this was that they had Tomo again. The Russians had brought him out from whatever corner they'd stashed him in, and besides a hefty lump on the back of his head, the third member of their party was little worse for the wear. Currently, he was running his comb through his hair.

Gunn was preoccupied, so Steiner had some minutes alone with the kid. He was taking a risk, trying to divide Tomo's allegiance. Gunn was right that they needed him, but Steiner would do all he could to save the boy's life. And for that, Tomo was going to need to be on Steiner's side.

"Tomo, listen," he said quietly, reigning in his fervent emotions so that the Russians wouldn't think they were conspiring. He smiled for their observers and glanced around, then leaned casually against a desk. "Tell me quickly, what do you think about what Gunn wants you to do?"

"I can't control it!"

"Keep it down. Act casual. Please. I don't think Gunn's making the best decisions now, and I have the beginnings of a plan. But I really need your help."

"Looks like *everyone* needs me now. *Gunn* wants to use me. *You* want to use me. I don't want to be *used*. I don't want to be in that monster's head anymore. I can't even function when it's around."

"I know. I'm sorry about all this." The doctor put his hand on Tomo's shoulder, no longer thinking about the Russians. "If I could be in your place, I *would* be."

"That would be crazy. Then *you* wouldn't be able to think when the monster's around—when we need you most."

"Still, I think much could be learned by getting into that monster's head, and you're the only one who can."

"I *can't*, I've told you. I mean, I think I can hear its thoughts or something *like* thoughts, but it cripples me every time."

The doctor looked up. Gunn was still talking to the people in charge and hadn't noticed them or didn't care. "Listen, about that...how bad is it now?"

"What do you mean? *You've* seen me! It's *bad*."

"But do you think it's getting better?"

"Have you been listening to me? How can I even *think* when that thing's in my head and my head feels like it's being slowly squeezed between two rifle butts?"

"But you know what to expect now. Do you think you could be more *alert* the next time?"

"I hope there *isn't* a next time!"

Dr. Steiner sighed. "I wish there wouldn't be, but I doubt it. See, Rex-1 is attached to you, kind of on a leash. It isn't going more than five miles away. It will always circle back."

"*Kuso!*" said Tomo.

Dr. Steiner pressed. "Please, Tomo, I know this isn't fair to ask you, but I need you to try to form a firmer link with Rex-1."

"Calling it that isn't going to make it seem less of a monster."

"Please, Tomo. Gunn is going to ask the same and more of you, but if we can appear to cooperate with him on this, it will buy me more time to figure out how we can use this to our advantage."

The flyboy stared at his hands on the edge of the desk. They were gripping it so hard their color had drained. With effort, he released his hold. "What do you need me to do?"

Gunn quickly saw the value in the little of their plan that they told him, and they were soon out in the open air again, ready to begin Dr. Steiner's experiment. Gunn stayed behind, but two soldiers accompanied them.

"What am I doing again?" Tomo asked nervously. He was sweating profusely already.

"First of all, try to relax and focus. Close your eyes. Don't worry. If we see the monster coming, we'll move fast."

Tomo obeyed.

"If you're nervous, it might feel it. Take deep breaths. Okay. Good. Now, call to it with your thoughts."

Tomo opened his eyes. "You *know* this is crazy. We're wasting time."

"Don't say that. I'm risking everything on this, and I have to believe it might work. If that brain can come to life after millions of years, anything's possible."

Tomo closed his eyes again and concentrated.

"Can you hear it?" Dr. Steiner asked. He prodded the flyboy with other questions. Did he feel anything foreign? Did he have an instinctual guess as to how far away the beast was? They even tried speaking to Rex-1, sending it telepathic messages of peace and safety.

There was nothing. For once, they wanted the beast, and it wouldn't come.

"It has to come back eventually," Dr. Steiner said wearily. "Keep trying."

Gunn's plan was painstakingly coming together. As Steiner worked with Tomo to draw the monster toward their trap, Gunn put together all the Russian he knew to get the weapons they would need. The Russians had to know the reason for everything, and he tried to be patient as he explained the diagram and the baseball-sized fusion reactor in a metal chest that had taken a lot of damage.

In the end, he'd exchanged his idea of blowing the bomb for this one. The problem with the first was simply that he couldn't figure out a way to *get* to the bomb. Tomo didn't have enough controlling ability. Steiner wasn't telling him anything.

But if they could surprise the monster—if Tomo could lull it into a false sense of security—they might catch the beast with its shirt off and get through the damaged plating to the reactor before the energy shield went up, assuming it still worked. They would have to be at a very close range. They would have only one chance. Their timing would have to be perfect to the second. If anyone shot too early, that window of opportunity would be lost. Of course, the best chance of success would be with the person who would be closest to the beast, the person controlling it, calling it, but he wasn't sure if he could trust a gun into the hands of Tomo, as nervous as the boy was. Either way, the boy was a necessary sacrifice. If he could, indeed, control the monster, he needed to call it as close as possible. He didn't see any way Tomo would escape as the beast came down. That was war.

Dr. Steiner had always known it was all about the head, the "key" to the project, as he'd once said. So, he was not surprised to find that his plans all fell along those lines. He had never even considered going for the fusion reactor or the nuclear bomb. Instinctively, he'd known it was the head they had to fight, and so he knew this thing with Tomo had to work. He only wished the kid could be left out of it entirely. The flyboy was scared, drained, barely hanging on. The doctor had failed his daughter. He felt a desperate need to protect this young soldier, in her stead.

Tomo was now lying on the ground, as still as death, trying to call the monster. A couple times, he had seemed to feel its presence, but he always pulled back in fear. He was giving all he dared. He could give more, but Steiner wouldn't force him.

It was time to try something new. The University of Moscow was sure to have what Steiner needed. Their microbots wouldn't be as advanced as his own. His expertise was the best in his field. Yet microbots were commonly used in scientific circles these days, and he was confident that it wouldn't take more than a little fiddling to adapt them to his needs.

The only problem with the university was the distance away. It was two or three miles, and perhaps that wasn't much in the grand scheme of things. Still, it would increase the monster's path of destruction by that much more, and more people would die.

Getting there was another matter. There might be a workable tank in the littered remains along the street, but the last time they had used a tank, the monster had found them. In the time it took to cross three miles of rubble in a tank, a lot could happen.

Eva woke up suddenly, fearing she had slept too long. They shouldn't be sleeping at all! What if the monster returned? They had to get back to her father. But how would they move? The Russian was too weak. He'd used all his strength to come for her. That thought warmed her from the base of her skull to the tips of her toes. She blushed. It was silly to be having girly feelings at a time like this. This man—Sasha—was in pain, and it was her turn to help him. It was just the thing to do. Nothing romantic about it. Still, she was almost afraid to touch him now, nevermind that she had been crushed against his chest moments before. She put an ear close to his mouth, listening for a breath. A faint stream of air escaped his slightly parted lips. She quickly looked away from his lips.

She had to clear her head. She had to *do* something. She was a doctor, after all. Not that kind of doctor, maybe, but she could do first aid, couldn't she? She looked at her companion with a more critical eye. He needed much more than first aid. The seriousness of the situation finally settling on her, she went to work, stripping bandages from her clothing— half of it was in tatters anyway—and binding the wounds on his legs tightly. He didn't stir, and that worried her.

When she was done, heedless of the blood on her hands, she tied the loose ends of her blouse together in the front, both to provide more cloth coverage where it mattered and to keep the tatters from scraping her already battered skin. Her midriff was completely exposed, but the air felt good on her burns. Good thing it wasn't cold. She had to chuckle to herself as she thought of an old, old movie, made before her grandfather was born, from the Century's Greatest Collection. What was it called? Oh, yes, *Star Wars*. There were nine movies, but she was thinking of the one where the beast in the arena conveniently ripped away the heroine's shirt to expose her midriff. Sexy even in battle. Eva felt anything but sexy now, despite the similarities.

She had taken off the Russian's jacket to work, and now she bundled it up and reached to put it under his head as a pillow. She jerked back in surprise as she met his opened eyes, and then carefully, embarrassed, she put the jacket under his head anyway. She froze as his fingers suddenly traced a line down her jaw. Unable to help herself, she leaned into his touch, grateful for the comfort she found there. And then, surprise upon surprise, he dropped his hand to her fingers, lifted them to his lips, and kissed them once, gently. She took it for the thank you it was and smiled tenderly down at him.

He continued to hold her hand, and by degrees, she became uncomfortable again with the intimacy. It awoke feelings in her that she didn't trust, and she stood up, breaking their contact, to assess their surroundings. She took a few steps away just for good measure. She was painfully aware that his eyes followed her. She must look a sight, half her clothes missing, blood smeared from head to toe. She sighed, and the Russian called her name. She turned to him.

He was signaling something, and she bent down to try to understand. He held his hands up to his ear like he was holding something. A phone? She didn't have one, and they weren't going to find a working one around here.

She shook her head and shrugged.

But his eyes turned more insistent. He continued his mime, this time making funny noises in the back of his throat. What did that sound like? Or was he trying to talk? Her look must have amused him because he chuckled. Then he began to speak in brief choppy sentences. She looked at him, completely bewildered. Was he going crazy? His sentences were punctuated by the strange noise in the back of his throat—like static— and then she understood.

"A radio! Of course!"

The Russian stopped his mime and smiled at her. Then he pointed through the rubble toward the half-collapsed entrance. He continued to mime, and she paid close attention this time, knowing he was telling her where she might find one. He pantomimed driving and jerked his torso this way and that. *Rough* driving. A tank? There were all sorts of military vehicles out there, most of them burned to ashes, but she might get lucky. He pointed to her, made his fingers walk away and then back, and pointed to himself. She should bring the radio back to him. Of course. She couldn't speak Russian, after all. She laughed at their method of communication, and he laughed with her.

Then before she went, she turned back to him, very carefully touched his knee where there weren't bandages, and looked up at him with concern. "Are you going to be okay?" she asked aloud.

He understood her meaning and nodded, shooing her away. He said something in Russian. She had no idea what it was but thought, by his look, that he might be telling her to be careful.

The air was clearer than it had been when she finally made it outside. Dark columns of smoke still rose intermittently in all directions, making the city look like a factory. But she could see between them into the sky, and it was impossible to miss the gigantic metal beast flying south.

***

Dr. Steiner was finally on the road, headed south to the university, and he was speaking into a radio. The Russians were finally cooperating, and it was easier to get things done. Granted, the frequency was short range and meant for communication with the base only, but that was all Steiner needed at the moment.

"General, what you want to do is suicide. Please let me get what I need before you do anything drastic," Steiner said over the radio.

Steiner was alone with two soldiers, one of whom was driving the tank. He'd wanted Tomo along. It would have made things much easier. But Gunn had plans for the flyboy, nevermind that the kid had little influence over the monster at this point. Now, the doctor had to get to the university and get back to the base with the supplies he needed to hook up his brain with Tomo's.

The upside to this arrangement was that the monster wouldn't get to push beyond its current five-mile boundary. Unfortunately, that five-mile boundary extended around the university, leaving Dr. Steiner's position as fragile as ever. He had to make it both directions without Rex-1 catching up. There was no question of attempting to escape the boundary completely. If they didn't destroy the monster *now*, Tomo was going to die eventually, and Steiner could only guess that the monster would be free, then, to destroy the world.

Gunn did not respond.

"General Gunn? General? Are you there?"

Static.

Dr. Steiner shrugged and put the radio aside. And then he heard a thunderous crash in the distance behind them.

Gunn was arguing with Dr. Steiner over the radio when two things happened at once. A soldier came flying into the war room, screaming unintelligibly, and Tomo grabbed his head and fell to one knee. Gunn needed only the second to understand what was happening. He grabbed Tomo by the shoulder and heaved him to his feet.

"Get a hold of yourself, soldier!" he yelled at the boy. "It's time!"

A noise like a freight train rumbled overhead, and cracks formed in the ceiling, causing dust to rain down around them. All remaining working monitors blinked off. Whatever had just happened outside, it had penetrated layers of concrete. The base wasn't so safe, after all.

Gunn yelled orders in Russian, and he was obeyed. It was clear who was in charge now—the one with the plan. Nobody else knew what to do.

Gunners ran for the surface, and the general dragged Tomo along with him.

"Focus, man! Focus!"

Tomo groaned but kept to his feet.

"Hurting, hurting," the flyboy murmured.

"I don't care!" Gunn yelled as they climbed the stairs.

"Hungry, hurting, bad things hurt—hurt *them*, KILL!" Tomo let out a feral roar that was echoed above, and Gunn halted at the top of the steps, true fear in his eyes as he looked into Tomo's empty ones. The kid wasn't controlling the beast, but the beast's mind had taken over the flyboy's. And the beast knew it had found its greatest enemy. The general ran from Tomo, machine gun in hand, and flew for the door. There was no more office building.

Gunn entered the murky shadow of the street and looked up and up the long scaled belly of the beast. There. Where the scales bent outward with previous damage was where the cold fusion reactor was. There was no way they were going to get to it. It had been a foolhardy plan, he now realized too late, yet what other option did they have but to go forward? Gunfire erupted without his signal. The general hardly noticed as he randomly pointed his own weapon upward and fired, a yell of defiance ripping from his throat. The beast roared again, and all Hell broke loose.

PART 3
By Timothy Deal

CHAPTER 12:
THE FIELD OF BATTLE

Sasha sat perfectly still, his ears straining to hear the distant booming. The shadow of the metal dragon had flown overhead just moments before, heading south. Then there had been the
echo of a dreadful crash followed by a series of explosions. The noises sounded far enough away that Sasha wasn't too worried about the blonde woman—Eva—for now, but he was beginning to suspect what place the monster had chosen for his new battleground.

The Russian carefully shifted his position, gritting his teeth as a wave of pain shot up his legs. He hoped he could still contact a nearby medical center if Eva found a radio. He needed to get some painkillers in him if he was going to make sure he could get the woman out of here alive. Not only that, but he also knew Eva's burns needed quick treatment to prevent permanent damage. For some reason, he couldn't bear the thought that her smooth skin might be forever scarred. After all that she had been through, such ruined beauty would be....

Sasha breathed a small chuckle. Why was he having these thoughts at a time like this? St. Basil's Cathedral lay in ruins around him; the whole world might be ending, for all he knew. He thought of his dead comrades, the fallen soldiers of the 521st Tank Brigade. They had been crushed, incinerated by a demon from Hell possibly summoned by their enemies. This woman, this Eva, she was on the enemy's side, wasn't she? Why should he care about her?

He touched his bandaged leg and studied the strips of cloth that Eva had carefully wrapped around his wounds. He realized he didn't have an answer to his question, but this didn't bother him. He had saved her; she had saved him. He had found something beautiful in her presence. That was all that mattered. For now, let politics be damned. He would protect her, however much he was able.

The garbled sounds of a radio speaker reached his ears and he quickly looked up. Eva was hurriedly making her way toward him, a handheld radio in her fist and a hopeful smile on her face. He smiled back and raised a hand in welcome. Eva knelt beside him and handed him the radio, saying words he couldn't understand. He raised a finger to his lips to silence her while he tried to hear what the voices on the radio were saying.

"...landed on top of the base and destroyed all satellite communications instantly..." one urgent voice said in Russian.

"—THE END! HOLY MOTHER OF—" screamed another Russian.

"...either back us up or stay the h...." Static interrupted a third Russian.

Sasha adjusted the frequency dial, trying to find a conversation with people that could help. From the bits of interchanges he heard, he gathered that the monster had attacked the government's secret base just south of their location, as he had suspected. He frowned in thought. If the Americans weren't controlling the monster anymore, how had it known to attack there?

Another voice crackled over the air, this time speaking an awkward Russian with an American accent: "Repeat, all men fire at center of enemy! The stomach! Fire at the stomach!"

Sasha instantly recognized the voice. His eyes connected with Eva's and he knew she recognized it too. The American general. Gunn.

With an ear-shattering cry of agony and rage, the monster whipped its tail into a line of supertanks that had been blistering the beast with their plasma shells. The impact sent the tanks toppling backwards like toy trucks, flattening anything and anyone in their path until they crashed into a nearby building. There the plasma cannons promptly exploded, blowing out the small building's remaining supports and sending its walls crashing into the ground.

The monster turned its gaze back toward the government base where a heavy artillery unit had emerged on the roof and was pelting the dragon's chest. Crimson beams burst from the monster's eyes, igniting the artillery unit in a giant fireball. The dragon then spewed a stream of fire onto the roof, as if it spitefully wanted to ensure the roof was turned into an inferno.

Meanwhile, Gunn and the remaining Russian infantrymen moved quickly around the giant's thundering footsteps as a military unit, careful not to be trampled as it fought. It was the first time in many years that Gen. Gunn had fought on the frontlines, but now as his blood boiled in the heat of combat, he felt many of his old instincts return to guide him across the battlefield—telling him when to dodge debris, when to take an opportunity to fire, when to duck for cover. So far his instincts had kept him alive…but they had never before been tested against a rampaging, gargantuan iron dragon.

"Incoming!" he bellowed, diving to his right.

A flaming hunk of metal crashed into the space where he had been standing. A Russian who had been running heedless of Gunn's warning nearly collided with the slab, but managed to stop himself just short of it. The man gaped at the fiery wreckage a fatal moment before a falling iron bar crushed his skull.

Gunn looked up and saw the beast—Apollyon, as Daniels had named him—ripping the Russian building apart with its bare claws, like a child eagerly unwrapping a present. Chunks of concrete and iron girders were falling like confetti. Gunn screamed in Russian, "Back! Back! Get away from the base!"

Soldiers fled in all directions away from the building. Some of them ran for blocks with no apparent intention of stopping until they were safe from the demon's wrath. Others found strategic hiding places around close corners and alleyways, still within firing range of the beast. Gunn joined these men while clutching his left side where a scrap of metal had been lodged.

"Graaaah!" he screamed as he slid the shrapnel free. He gripped his side with his left hand, trying to keep the bleeding to a minimum while he used his other hand to tear cloth from his shirt. One of the soldiers nearby stooped to help him and together they wound a bandage of torn clothes around his middle. Panting, Gunn nodded at the soldier and thanked him.

The solider nodded back but continued to look at Gunn in anticipation. The general realized that several of the nearby Russians were now looking at him, waiting for their orders. He swallowed, though it didn't help the hard dryness in his mouth. Warriors needed a leader in times like this, and Gunn was the only one around for these men. He looked up at the monster and gritted his teeth.

"The middle," he said in Russian. He pointed toward the belly of the beast where some of its organic scales and exo-armor had been peeled back by plasma blasts. "If we focus enough fire at the middle, the stomach, we may kill it. That's the weak spot."

It was a long shot. Even the combined machine and plasma gunfire of all the remaining Russians didn't have a great chance of penetrating deep enough into Rex-1's body to set off the fusion reactor. Yet it was the only hope Gunn could see at this moment, and it was the only hope that he could give. The soldiers seized on it and turned back toward the beast with a renewed fire in their eyes.

But fire was also still in the eyes of Apollyon as it turned its attention from the smoldering ruins of the government building to the soldiers in the street. Those who had heard Gunn's instructions screamed in defiance and rage. They poured gunfire into the beast's belly, generating a fireworks display of sparks and flashes. The dragon took a step back and made a low, rumbling sound. That sound was the threatening growl of a beast, and it quickly escalated into a deafening roar as the dragon lunged forward with a rush of fire blasting from its mouth. Soldiers leapt out of the way, though some were caught up in the explosions of ignited cars and gas lines.

As Apollyon began marching down the street toward the fleeing soldiers, knocking down buildings that were in its way, Gunn pried a radio from a dead Russian's hand and took it down a nearby alleyway. He pressed the talk button and screamed into the radio as he ran. "Attention! All men, anyone within firing range!" he cried. "Fire at the center of enemy! Repeat, all men fire at center of enemy! The stomach! Fire at the stomach!"

Gunn rounded a corner and looked down the street to see the monster stalking its prey at the other end of the block. Aiming his gun into the belly of the beast, the general emptied a round without even attracting the dragon's attention. Gunn grunted as he reloaded his weapon. He was raising it to fire again when an American woman's voice came through his radio speaker. "General Gunn, is that you? Is my father there? ...Hello?"

Gunn ducked back behind the building and stared at his radio. Dr. Steiner's daughter? He pressed the talk button. "Miss Steiner?" he said.

"Yes! Yes, it's me!" The voice on the other end sounded excited to have found contact. "Is my father with you, General Gunn?"

"No! No, he's not! He went to the University of Moscow to pick up some materials he thought might help defeat the mon...defeat Rex-1." Gunn knew now that he had made Dr. Steiner create a demon of a monster, but he wasn't ready to admit that to anyone. There was too much at stake to let himself be burdened with guilt right now. Meanwhile, the prospect of Dr. Steiner creating another way to take down the beast sounded very appealing. "Where are you, Miss Steiner?"

"We're at Saint Basil's Cathedral, or what's left of it anyway."

"Is Daniels with you?"

"He was." The sudden coldness in Eva's voice was obvious even over the radio. "I'm hoping he's rotting in Hell or a very, very long Purgatory right now."

Gunn raised an eyebrow but decided to ask a different question for the moment. "Then who's with you now?"

Eva's voice turned warm again as she replied, "Sasha. Our Russian tank driver."

Gunn frowned. "Has he done anything to you? Anything suspicious?"

"Quite the contrary. He saved me from a madman. Now general, are you sure my father is safe?"

The general peeked around the corner and saw the dragon's head towering above buildings further down the street. "I'm reasonably sure, Miss Steiner," Gunn replied as he began walking quickly after the beast. "Rex-1 is currently headed in the opposite direction of the university. We should be able to keep it occupied until your father has put together his plan. You should stay hidden for now."

"Wait, general, in which direction did you say the monster is headed?"

"North. Possibly toward you. Stay hidden. Over and out." Gunn clipped the radio onto his belt and began to run as fast as his injuries would let him.

CHAPTER 13:
THE SHADOW OF THE FALLEN

Dr. Steiner and his Russian escorts strode quickly into the university science building. Glancing down the hallways, one of the Russians asked his compatriot something. The other Russian made a reply and pointed to a wall directory. The pair began to study the directory, leaving Dr. Steiner to look around the atrium anxiously.

Gunn had told the escorts to take Dr. Steiner to the robotics division of the university science department, but the soldiers didn't have any better idea of where that was than he did. It had taken them precious time to get this far. "Please hurry!" Dr. Steiner told his escorts, hoping that the urgency in his voice would get through.

The two Russians looked at him and seemed to understand. They nodded at him, turned back to the directory, and conferred with each other hurriedly. Then they beckoned the doctor toward one of the hallways and began to run that direction. Dr. Steiner followed, praying that he would be able to find what he needed to end this madness.

Gunn's words left Eva dumbstruck for several moments. Then she turned toward Sasha, who was anxiously watching her and waiting for explanation. "It's…" she started, but faltered as her heart thumped in her ears. She took a deep breath and steeled herself. Pointing toward the increasingly loud explosions and thunderous crashes, Eva said, "It's coming…" She pointed to the ground. "…here."

Sasha's eyes hardened. He immediately put a hand against the wall he had been leaning against and tried to raise himself to his feet. Eva rushed to his side and helped him up. "Easy… easy," she said. "Sasha." The Russian looked into her face. Eva exhaled and said, "We need to hide."

She pointed at the two of them and slipped a hand over her face. She peeked out over the top of her hand and then brought her eyes back down, like a parent playing peek-a-boo. Sasha chuckled and then stopped himself and nodded. Smiling again at the awkwardness of their communication, Eva then pointed further into the church ruins.

With Sasha leaning on Eva for support, the pair slowly limped their way through the ruins of the cathedral. Eva looked for an exit from the sanctuary area that led into one of the side hallways, but she didn't see a doorway that wasn't demolished or blocked by rubble. Sasha gestured toward the still-standing sidewall where a confessional stood relatively unharmed. Eva nodded. "That'll work," she said.

Eva helped Sasha toward the confessional and opened the door. She guided the Russian inside first and then followed, shutting the door behind her. There wasn't much room in the wooden box for both of them to sit, so Eva let Sasha rest on the bench while she stood. She considered entering the priest's side of the confessional, but what if Sasha needed help getting out quickly? It would be better if they stayed together.

They stayed motionless for several minutes, their eyes adjusting to the darkness, their ears straining to hear and understand the noises coming from some distance away outside. They heard the echoing crashes of concrete against concrete, the rumbling of heavy debris, the shattering booms of explosions, the pattering of angry gunfire, and, above all, the bellowing roar of a fearsome beast. These sounds were faint at first, but as Eva and Sasha listened, the sounds continued to grow unmistakably louder. The tumultuous crashing that had seemed a mile away when they first started looking for a hiding place now thundered close at hand, perhaps only a block away from the ruins of St. Basil's Cathedral.

Sasha took Eva's hand. She started a little in surprise, but then realized she had been trembling. She stared into his eyes for a moment and saw fear, concern...and a yearning desire to protect them both. Sasha pushed himself into the corner of the confessional and pulled Eva closer to him. She squeezed herself next to him on the bench and leaned against his shoulder, the close quarters only encouraging her need for human touch. With his hand still holding hers, Sasha tenderly stroked her skin with his thumb. Eva reached for his other hand, and he gave it to her. They leaned against each other now, their hands clasped together, the din of destruction roaring outside.

Eva closed her eyes and tried to block out the stomach-churning sounds of twisting metal and tumbling buildings. She tried to focus on the touch of Sasha's large, rough hands in her smooth, more delicate ones. But the sounds of battle were deafening now, and Eva found she couldn't bear to keep her eyes closed for fear of not knowing what was coming. Without moving from Sasha's side, she tried to peer through the cracks of the confessional. She caught her breath. Was that a shadow that just passed over the church ruins?

Suddenly, there was a series of loud shrieks of metal against pavement outside followed by a nearby crash that sent an avalanche of bricks, wood, and stone hurtling into the confessional door. Eva screamed as she and Sasha pulled their feet on top of the bench as the door and walls of the wooden box caved into the floor, burying the bottom two meters of the confessional area with rubble.

A cloud of dust settled, and for a brief moment, the only sound Eva could hear over her ringing ears was that of her and Sasha's coughing. She looked down. A small pile of bricks and broken concrete had poured over the top of the bench, scraping her feet and ankles, but otherwise, she hadn't been hurt. She looked at Sasha with concern. He kicked a brick off his foot and grimaced a little. Then he turned with full attention toward Eva and asked her something worriedly. Eva nodded and smiled weakly to reassure him. She was about to reply when a quivering voice interrupted.

"Heyyy…it's-it's ah…Goldie Locks!"

Eva turned toward the voice and gasped. Even amid the cloud of dust, she could make out the twisted form of a military jeep sticking out from underneath the rubble of what used to be the last standing wall of the cathedral. Standing on top of the wreckage was Tomo. His hair was uncharacteristically disheveled. Blood stained his hands and flightsuit and was flowing unchecked from his nose. His face was constantly twitching, seemingly contorting his facial expression between anger and pleasure. He cackled and swept his arm in a wide arc. "C-come sssee—gak—whaat I-I-I found!" he cried.

"What happened to him?" Eva whispered. "Did his mental connection drive him mad?"

Though he couldn't have known exactly what she said, Sasha grunted suspiciously and painfully dragged himself to his feet. "Careful!" Eva exclaimed, clutching his arm. "You're not steady on your legs yet!"

Sasha ignored her and put himself between Tomo and Eva. He yelled something threatening to Tomo whose expression turned horrifying. "DAMN RUSSIAN!" he screamed.

A sudden thud nearby sent shockwaves into the ground, causing Eva and Sasha to stumble for their balance. With a cry of pain, Sasha tumbled onto his side. Eva knelt beside him and cried out his name. Sasha only looked above her head with fear and dread in his eyes. Eva stopped breathing, knowing what he saw, but unable to keep herself from turning to follow his gaze.

There was Apollyon, staring straight at them.

Eva screamed. Sasha struggled to get back to his feet. Apollyon reached toward them, his claws scraping the ground. Eva stood transfixed, stunned, until Sasha tugged at her arm and woke her up. She turned to run and shouted for Sasha to do the same.

She was too late. Apollyon's fingers blocked her path and began to close around her. Her scream faded into a gasp as the fingers began to press against her body, making it difficult to breathe. Sasha screamed something in Russian and jammed a metal bar into the monster's metal finger joints. The squeezing stopped momentarily, giving Eva a chance to wiggle her way into some breathing room. "Sasha! No! Get away from here!" she shouted.

An unearthly growl emanated from the dragon's throat. It drew its head back, as if preparing to unleash an inferno of fire, but at a cry from Tomo, it stopped. Eva shot a glance toward the flyboy and saw him holding his head in concentration, the bizarre expressions still twisting themselves across his face. Then she suddenly realized the monster's eyes had begun to glow a bright red. Eva screamed at Sasha, "DUCK! HIDE!"

Sasha had already seen it coming and dove to the ground, avoiding Apollyon's lasers by centimeters. A cry of frustration from Tomo gave Eva an idea. "Leave him alone!" she cried, both at Tomo and at the monster. "You can take me wherever you like, but leave him alone! He means no harm!"

Heedless of her cries, the dragon swung its free hand toward Sasha where he lay prone on the ground. "NO! STOP!"

The claws froze in midair, dangling above Sasha's head. Tomo stared at Eva, his face rapidly flipping through emotions. Eva swallowed and tried to control her panting. Tears were streaming down her face now, and her voice cracked as she said, "Please stop. He's my friend."

Tomo scrunched his eyes shut and began to twist his head from side to side. He groaned and screamed as his body shook for a full minute. The monster seemed equally agitated; deep murmurs and snarls emanated from its mouth as it waited, its claws hanging over Sasha, Eva still in its grip.

Suddenly, a shower of gunfire began to pelt the dragon's back. Tomo straightened up and ran toward the beast. Apollyon roared, snatched Tomo up in its free hand, and spread its wings. "No! No, wait!" Eva cried.

Again she was too late. With a mighty leap, the dragon took to the sky, a tortured boy in one claw and a terrified woman in the other.

CHAPTER 14:
RETREAT AND REFORM

Sasha stared at the retreating form of the dragon until it swooped around one of the few tall buildings still standing and was lost from sight. Emptiness descended into Sasha's heart. He turned his stare to the ground and wondered if this battle was worth the anguish. Would they have been better off surrendering when the monster came to land? Should they have just given themselves up to death?

Then Sasha thought of Eva's soft touch, her hopeful smile, and her gentle laughter. Should the world be robbed of such a person? Sasha set his teeth. If there was a chance he could save her, the battle was still worth fighting.

"Comrade!"

Sasha sat up and saw a group of soldiers making their way into the ruins of the cathedral. Some of them came toward him and knelt beside him, asking how badly he was hurt. "I've been bandaged up pretty well," Sasha told his fellow Russians in his native tongue, "but I need a painkiller right away. Anybody have one?"

"Yes, sir!" One of the men dug into his pockets. "There was an overturned ambulance not far from the base. I took the opportunity to grab a bunch of them. Figured we'd need it."

The man pulled out a handful of plastic bags, each one containing a covered syringe filled with liquid. "Anyone here a medical specialist?" Sasha asked. The men around him shook their heads. Sasha studied the bag labels and said, "No matter. It looks like most of these are the same, anyway."

Sasha picked out two bags and gave each to a different soldier. They opened the bags, uncovered the syringes, and looked at Sasha. He lay back down and said, "I'm ready."

The two men stuck a syringe in each leg and began to empty the liquid inside. Sasha gritted his teeth while the pain in his legs enflamed anew with such intensity, it felt as if his skin was burning below the surface. Then his legs began to grow numb, and the pain gradually subsided. Within a minute, his legs weren't hurting at all. Sasha hurriedly climbed to his feet.

Gunn, the American general, was there watching him. "You do know," the general said in his broken Russian, "that is not a permanent fix, correct? Your legs are still healing. You are not fit for action."

Sasha glowered and strode in front of Gunn. He looked down into the older man's face and said, "Your monster has Eva. I will save her and then send that beast back to Hell, where it belongs."

Gunn looked away and sighed. Then he turned back to Sasha and said, "Your choice, soldier. If you go into battle now, your legs will suffer serious permanent damage. Your life in the military will be over."

Sasha grunted and turned in the direction the dragon had flown. "Right now, I couldn't care less."

Eva clung to the monster's iron finger like she was clinging onto life. A rational voice inside her head told her that probably wasn't necessary; the dragon's fingers had her pinned pretty tight. But practical reason didn't seem very persuasive when she was being carried by a raging metal dragon hundreds of feet off the ground.

Apollyon suddenly banked left, causing Eva to shriek in surprise. A plasma shell flew past them and exploded in empty air, close enough that Eva could feel its heat. Her eyes searched the ground, trying to find the source, but at this height it was hard to find a tank amid all the buildings. Apparently, the monster didn't see it either, or it didn't care. It blasted a fireball randomly downward and swirled around back to its original flight path.

Eva clutched her mouth, trying to hold back nausea. She was used to most air travel, but the unorthodox swoops the dragon made unnerved her stomach. The fear gnawing inside her didn't help. Maybe a distraction would.

"Hey, Tomo," Eva called out weakly. "Where are we going? Where's it taking us?"

The young pilot looked at her with a crazed grin and made a sound somewhere between a cough and a laugh. Then he called back, "Sssssafffeuh. Sssommmeplace where we'llllllllll—cak, cak—be saaaffffffe."

"Safe? Tomo, I'd be safer down on the ground!"

"Nooo, no no no no! Crazy, MEAN! Russians! They HURT ussss!" Tomo's expressions twitched violently. One second he was grinding his teeth in a fierce scowl, the next his jaw had dropped and his eyes were wide in fear. "Nooo more! FINISH this! Keep us saaafe!"

Now that the monster was in the sky again, there was time to put together a better plan. Gunn began to ask the Russians if anyone was carrying or had seen a usable bazooka. He knew all missile launch points had already been destroyed—he'd seen to it personally in the Nighthawk. But he was certain that if he could get a good bazooka at the right elevation, he could put a guided shell straight through the crater in Rex-1's armor and into the fusion reactor.

Of course, if the fusion reactor was hit, the resulting explosion would likely start a chain reaction that would set off the nuclear warhead, erasing

Moscow off the map. It was still a sacrifice Gunn was willing to make. Since the doctor had only been able to take a shortwave radio with him, there was no telling if he had made any progress on his alternate plan, and Gunn had no time to wait. Now that the dragon was flying around with Tomo, they had to take it out before it discovered it could leave the city.

None of the first dozen men had seen a bazooka. Gunn started walking toward another group of soldiers, who were conversing worriedly, when a civilian truck pulled into his path. The Russian tank driver—Sasha, apparently—gazed at Gunn from the driver's seat. "Your Japanese man's gone mad," he said in Russian. "Do you know why?"

Gunn sighed and searched for the right words. "He has a mental...connection with the... monster," he said. He hated calling it a monster, but he didn't know any other Russian words to describe it. "He got too close to it back at the secret base. I think the monster's been controlling his mind ever since."

Still holding his gaze, Sasha said, "Perhaps. I heard you were looking for a good bazooka. Why? What will a bazooka do that our supertanks could not?"

Gunn hesitated, but remembered that he could use whatever help he could get. "One of the plasma shells tore open a hole in its armor. It exposed its weak spot. If I can get a bazooka high enough, I should be able to hit the target and stop the monster."

"What about Eva?"

That's right; the rugged tank driver had seemingly taken a liking to Eva. Gunn had better put this carefully. "She should be safe, as long as the monster is on the ground. She won't be hurt."

"And if the monster is flying? What then?" Sasha eyed Gunn suspiciously

"We...we'll figure something out," Gunn replied. He needed the Russian to work with him on this. "But we're running out of time. Did you find a bazooka?"

Sasha hesitated a moment, but then frowned and nodded. He jerked a thumb over his shoulder and said, "Back seat. Found it in the cathedral ruins. It must have fallen out of the jeep when it crashed. You want in?"

"You believe it, soldier. But wait just a moment."

Gunn climbed onto the back of the truck and shouted some orders to the nearby soldiers. Any man who could find transportation was to follow his truck as they trailed the monster. They would need to lay a distracting cover fire while he set up the finishing blow. Filled with the hope that this nightmare would soon be over, the soldiers scrambled to find their place in nearby cars or motorcycles that still worked. Gunn climbed into the passenger side of Sasha's truck.

"One warning," Sasha said, looking sideways at the general. "I've seen how you treat your comrades, and I don't trust you. If I find you're attempting to destroy the monster by sacrificing Eva in the process…I'll kill you."

The threat lingered in the air like a thundercloud. Gunn turned his eyes toward the road and muttered, "Just drive."

CHAPTER 15:
BRUTE FORCE

A caravan of cars, trucks, jeeps, and motorcycles sped through the streets of Moscow. Following the direction Apollyon had taken, they made their way northwest, impeded occasionally by rubble, though never by traffic. Gunn had sent a truckload of men to follow Apollyon as soon as it had taken flight, and now the caravan followed their route, indicated by distinct lines of machine gunfire on the buildings they passed. They had only gone a few miles when cries began emerging from the troops, and soon everyone realized where their destination lay.

Ahead of them loomed Triumph Palace, a towering monument to 21st century architecture encompassing several connected buildings of lavish residential space. In the center, flanked by two skyscrapers, the main tower rose over the rest of the Palace at a height over 860 feet. At the very top of this tower perched Apollyon, his wings unfurled, his clawed hands clenched as he surveyed the city, seemingly daring a challenger to come to him.

As the caravan emerged into the streets surrounding the Palace, Apollyon made a roar that seemed a shout of pleasure as much as it was a war cry. It hurled a stream of fire to the ground, igniting buildings and the trees of a nearby park. The fire also fell across the road in front of the Palace, bringing the caravan to a halt.

Sasha leaned forward, trying to see the top of the skyscraper. His eyes were wide with fear and worry as he said, "Do you see her? Do you Eva up there?"

Gunn didn't respond. He had already jumped out of the truck and begun shouting orders to the soldiers behind them. Some of the men started piling out of their vehicles and began to run into the surrounding buildings, both for the shelter they provided and to get a higher shot at the monster. Others remained in their vehicles, preparing their weapons to fire at the monster while they were on the move.

Sasha saw the dragon descend to one of the lower buildings of the Palace and look toward the caravan with crimson eyes. "Incoming!" Sasha bellowed, bolting from the truck.

Apollyon's laser beam gaze cut through the truck Sasha had been in, as well as a jeep that had been behind it. Both burst into flame, sending hunks of metal flying in all directions. The remaining drivers in the caravan immediately took off, going in separate directions to prevent becoming a big target. With street space limited, some tore through the park landscape, swerving around burning trees and park benches as they launched plasma fire onto the dragon.

Sasha looked around for Gunn, but the general was nowhere to be seen. With a curse, Sasha began running toward the closest entrance to Triumph Palace. The monster wasn't holding Eva in its clutches. Maybe she was on top of the building. If not...Sasha couldn't think about it. Grasping at hope, he kept running.

"Hehehehhh...burn. BURN! Fffinnnissssh you ALL!"

Tomo was standing at the edge of the tower rooftop, watching the destruction several hundred feet below. His expressions now appeared more triumphant and angry than terrified, though he still twitched violently, and his eyes were invariably wide open. He cackled and turned toward the observation area. "Cooool, huh, Goldie-hach!-locks?"

Eva pushed one more time at the iron bars that held her in place, but it was no use. The monster had pulled the protective railings tight across her middle, pinning her arms, chest, and stomach to one of the pillars that circled the observation area. All her struggling hadn't budged the bars an inch. Eva sagged against the railings, panting from her efforts. "Tomo, why are you doing this?" Eva said, gasping. "Let me go!"

He shook his head fiercely. "No, no no no baby! Can't d-d-do thaaat. Keep you saaaafe. Youuuu can't ra-ra-ra-raACH! Can't run ah-aoff. Mean mennn—RUSSIANS! They HURT YOU! NOT saaaaffe."

"Tomo, that-that thing, that monster, that's what's dangerous! You can't let it control you! You've got to stop it!"

Her words seemed to set off fireworks in Tomo's brain. He screamed in agony and clutched his head. Convulsing more violently than ever, he fell to the rooftop and kept screaming as his eyes stared agape and the veins on his forehead throbbed. Alarmed, Eva called out his name.

Tomo's trembling gradually subsided into a mild shudder. He looked up into Eva's eyes, making her gasp. His brow was still scrunched together in pain and his right cheek twitched, but his eyes were clear and his smile was familiar. He spoke with a strained voice, "I'm still here, babe. Still Tomo. I'm trying to control the beastie, but—gruh!" Tomo's eyes snapped shut against the pain. "But it ain't as easy as it looks. I send it suggestions. That's about all I can manage—GRAAAH!" The flyboy curled into a fetal position and wheezed for breath. He looked back at Eva imploringly and croaked, "Where's your dad?"

Eva stared at him helplessly. She shook her head and felt tears pool in her eyes. "I-I don't know," she said.

Footsteps resounded on the spiral staircase behind her. Someone was coming onto the observational deck! Eva caught her breath and tried to crane her neck around the pillar, but she couldn't see the staircase. Then a masculine voice echoed in the tower, "Eva! Eva!"

Eva's heart leapt. Sasha! He had found her! "Yes! Sasha!" she screamed. "Up here!"

"Eva!"

Sasha's voice emerged out of the staircase. She heard his footsteps on the floor behind her. Suddenly, Tomo jumped to his feet and snarled. The sanity was gone from his face, replaced by pulsating rage. "YOU!" he screamed. "Ssshould have KILLED!"

Tomo leapt behind Eva's pillar toward the footsteps. "No! Tomo!" Eva cried. "Stop!"

There was a short scuffle and the sound of a gun falling down the metal staircase before Tomo was suddenly flung back to the edge of the roof. Sasha stepped into Eva's view, shaking the tension out of his hand and panting furiously. Tomo stood again and rushed at Sasha with a shriek.

Sasha heaved a punch at Tomo's gut, but the agile flyboy caught the Russian's fist in his. In the next second, Tomo had swung his leg into the Russian's head, dazing the larger man enough to sink him to his knees. The flyboy tore into Sasha then, pummeling him with a furious stream of punches, karate chops, and kicks. The Russian took the abuse for half a minute before regaining his senses. With a roar that drowned out Tomo's enraged screams, Sasha used a backhanded fist to bash Tomo backward. Standing up, Tomo raised his fists like a trained boxer and lunged forward.

Eva stared transfixed at the scene as the Russian and the Japanese American brawled atop the skyscraper, a robotic demon unleashing an inferno on Moscow behind them. Blood splattered the sides of the men's faces even as the blast of nearby explosions shook the air. Eva imagined she could almost hear Daniels muttering feverishly in her ear, "And the brother shall deliver the other brother to death...For nation shall rise against nation, and kingdom against kingdom...All these are the beginning of sorrows."

Eva shuddered at the memory of the priest, but she refused to let her fear overcome her. "Stop!" she shouted at the clashing men. "Sasha, Tomo, stop! This isn't helping!"

Sasha paused to look at her. In that instant, Tomo's fist smashed into Sasha's face, knocking him backward toward the edge of the roof. The soldier's foot slipped into empty space, and Sasha fell, barely managing to grab onto the rooftop edge with his fingertips. Eva screamed Sasha's name. Tomo's face was a swirl of emotions, flipping between demented triumph to pain-wracked concern within seconds. "NOW," he proclaimed, "I-I-I thhhink you're about t-t-to diiiiiiieeee! Ssssssorrry."

Suddenly, a missile exploded right beside Apollyon's head, flooding the high area with intense light. A startled cry burst from Tomo's mouth but was quickly cut short as the flyboy froze in place as if he had been turned to stone.

The ground forces let up on their gunfire. The men stared at the dragon from behind their guns. Unbelievably, the missile those two soldiers had brought had stunned the monster. It slowly moved its head from side to side as if it was in a trance. The men looked at each other. If the missile was successful, they had been ordered not to fire unless the dragon resumed its attack. Should they waste this opportunity to finish it off? Unease filled the air. No one seemed ready to invoke the demon's wrath, so they waited.

CHAPTER 16:
MIND OVER MATTER

Eva blinked painfully as the bright light began to fade. What on earth had happened? As her sight returned, she saw an older man wearing a pilot's helmet helping Sasha back to the rooftop. Once Sasha was safe, the older man quickly turned back to Tomo. Pilot sunglasses covered the man's eyes, but Eva would know that face anywhere. New life sprang into her eyes as she cried out, "Dad!"

Dr. Steiner practically jumped. He whirled toward Eva, pulled his glasses off, and gaped at her in joy and amazement. "Eva! Eva!" he cried. "My god, you're alive! I thought you were dead! Oh, my god!" He leapt to her side and touched her cheek. "You are real," he whispered unbelievingly. His eyes fell to the metal trapping his daughter. "Are you okay? Are you hurt?"

"I'm alive. I'm okay for now," Eva answered breathlessly. She nodded toward Tomo. "But what about them? The monster?"

Dr. Steiner's face grew grim again. "Yes, I can't stop now. If we survive this, Eva…." Dr. Steiner swallowed, fighting back his emotions. "We'll make it. By God, we'll make it."

The doctor rushed back to Tomo and pushed a sequence of buttons on the side of his helmet. Placing his hands on Tomo's shoulders, Dr. Steiner said, "Don't worry, son. Soon this will all be over."

An uneasy feeling crept over Eva. "Wait, Dad, what are you doing?"

"I found all the materials I needed at the university, Eva," Dr. Steiner replied as his helmet began to hum. "Better than I could have hoped for. I'm going to try to relieve Tomo of his mental link. I'm going to take control of Rex-1 myself."

"No! Dad!" Eva's eyes widened in panic. "The mental link drove Tomo crazy! You won't be able to control it!"

The helmet was buzzing now. Dr. Steiner's cheeks had begun to quiver, but he managed to send his daughter an encouraging smile. "Don't worry. I created this monstrosity, remember? If anyone can tell it to stop functioning, I can."

Apollyon was stirring. It placed its claws against the tower like it was bracing itself against an invisible foe. Dr. Steiner's face was clenched in concentration. "Microbot surgery, sixty-four percent," he muttered. "The flash implant was successful, but brain override is taking longer than estimated. Come on, little robots, secure the frequency!"

Looking confused by Dr. Steiner's methods, Sasha turned to Eva and examined her metal bonds. He said something with concern to her, but she didn't respond. Her eyes were locked on her father. Dr. Steiner was groaning under the strain now, his eyes blinking painfully behind lowered eyebrows.

Apollyon thrashed its head from side to side, ripping huge dents in the side of the building with each turn. Roaring defiantly, it turned to face the tower and began to sink its claws into the building's side. Hand over claw, it began to scale the surface of the Palace, its mighty wings forgotten in its turmoil. Finally, its crowned head peeked over the edge of the observation deck, and it scowled at its creator. Apollyon's eyes burned red.

"No, you won't," muttered Dr. Steiner through gritted teeth. "Go back down and express your pain."

Apollyon paused. The monster and the scientist stared at each other. Each moment seemed like an hour to Eva as she watched in silent terror. Eventually, the dragon accepted the doctor's suggestion and descended back to its perch on the lower skyscraper. Then, raising its head to the sky it roared once more, a cry of anguish and confusion, as well as anger.

Dr. Steiner took a deep breath. "Microbot surgery, seventy-eight percent! Almost there!" The doctor winced as he fidgeted with a handheld readout. He called out to Eva with a voice straining to make out the words, "I've suppressed—eeragh!—most of the monster's instincts—uhhhah!—so I have firm control of it. Hrrrngh! I'm going to disconnect...Tomo's connection now. He may fall—unconscious—ah!—but he should be all right. See if you can get that...Russian man to help him."

Eva nodded anxiously. "Whatever you say, Dad."

She looked at Sasha who had just retrieved his plasma gun from the staircase. She beckoned toward Tomo with her eyes. Still looking confused, Sasha approached Tomo but kept his distance.

The doctor took another breath and squeezed his eyes shut. Tomo began to slump to the ground, prompting Sasha to catch him and gently lower him down. Dr. Steiner's head jerked as he panted, "Much...harder...now...eighty-three percent."

Apollyon slammed its head against the tower, furious at the pain that buzzed inside its head. The tower quaked at the impact, and Dr. Steiner and Sasha stumbled for their footing. "Easy... easy," Dr. Steiner murmured. "It will be—gruh—over soon. Almost...what's...that noise?"

The whirling beat of helicopter blades was making its way toward Triumph Palace. Apollyon turned and growled at the new threat. The doctor took an intake of breath. "Nooo, nottt nowww!" he exclaimed.

A tethered man was leaning out of the helicopter as it approached the metal dragon. It was Gunn, his face hard and full of determination. He unslung a bazooka from his shoulder and took careful aim at Apollyon.

"What is he doing?" Eva exclaimed. "Where did he find a working helicopter?"

"Hospital," Dr. Steiner gasped. "Noottt nowww, YOU FOOL! I c-c-can handle this!"

Apollyon spewed a stream of fire at the oncoming enemy. The helicopter suddenly dropped in elevation, barely evading the attack. The dragon directed its fire down after it and the helicopter banked to its right, remaining just short of the blast. A bazooka shell flew from the chopper and into the tower above the dragon's head, showering it with dust and debris. Growling, Apollyon batted boulders of concrete away from its head while the aircraft moved in for the kill.

"Nooo! Yyyou'll KILL US ALL!" Dr. Steiner bellowed.

Sasha saw what was happening and leveled his plasma gun. He muttered to himself in Russian, "I warned you, general."

Gunn was bearing a grim, stoic expression as he aimed his bazooka at the crater in the dragon's armor. "This is for Daniels," he muttered and squeezed the trigger. In that same instant, he took a blast of plasma to the face.

The bazooka shell went hurtling toward Apollyon's weak point, hitting the edge of the crater. Both monster and creator howled in pain as the explosion ripped out more of the cyborg's exo-armor, dropping a hailstorm of broken metal upon the ground. Dr. Steiner fell to his knees and ripped the helmet off his head. "Dad!" Eva called out, her face white. "What's going on? Are you all right?"

"T-t-t-oo dangerous to c-c-continue," Dr. Steiner replied with heaving breaths and a raspy voice. "B-b-brain overrrrride fffinished at eighty-eight percent."

The doctor paused and looked glassy-eyed toward the monster. A myriad of sparks was dancing over Apollyon's chest. It sat on its building slumped against the main tower, its head twitching and growling in continuing agony. The doctor stared at the beast for several more minutes, lost in thought.

"Is it safe?" Eva asked. "What was Gunn trying to do?"

Dr. Steiner didn't break his gaze as he replied, "Destroy the cold fffusion reactor innn Rex-1. That or iggn-ignite the nuclear warhead inside. Both w-would have the same resultsss, really."

"Nuclear warhead!" Eva's heart sank to new depths. "Dad, I thought you got rid of that."

The doctor clenched his fists. "I DID. Ssssomebody put it back in." He sighed and turned toward his daughter "T-too late now. I'm sssorry, Eva, but I'mmm going to have to leave you n-now."

Apollyon rose, unfurled its wings, and ascended to the observation deck. Settling down on the roof, the beast directed its attention toward Eva. She squeezed her eyes shut, not bearing to meet its gaze. Suddenly, she felt a great weight lifted from her. She opened her eyes and saw the dragon had unwrapped the iron bars from around her body. Stiffly, she walked forward and into the arms of her father, who gripped her tightly in a hug. "Easy, Dad," Eva said with an exhausted chuckle. "I just got free. I don't want to be squeezed that hard anytime soon."

"Goodbye, Eva," Dr. Steiner said, stroking her hair. "Always remember that I love you."

Eva drew back in alarm. "Wait, Dad, what's going on? Why are you saying this?"

Dr. Steiner let his daughter go and went to the dragon's side. "A ch-chain reaction hasss been set off. I have to get Rex-1 out of here before the nuke goes off. I love you, Eva."

Apollyon's hand closed around Dr. Steiner's body just tight enough to secure him for flight. Fear and panic welled in Eva's throat, and she ran toward her father screaming, "No! There has to be another way! Dad, you can't die! You've already saved us!"

The dragon rose into the air, out of Eva's reach. Dr. Steiner looked down remorsefully at his daughter. "I'm only p-p-paying the price for my ssssin. You were rrrright, Eva. We should never have built this thing. B-but now, we're going to settt it right." Wincing from the mental connection, he looked up at the monster's head and said, "Let's end your pain, Rex-1."

The dragon turned and began to ascend as it flew northeast. Eva screamed after them, "No! Dad! Dad! Don't leave me!"

Dr. Steiner's voice called back, "Goodbye, Eva! I'm sssorry for everything! Goodbye!"

Eva fell to the floor and let out the piercing wail of one whose world had crumbled.

Miles of landscape flew past as the dragon hurtled through the air. Wind whipped past Dr. Steiner's face, which was tight with concentration. It felt like he was mentally holding the cyborg together, trying to keep all the internal systems from combusting until they were far enough away from civilization. Rex-1's mechanisms were screeching and cracking at the strain, but the doctor pushed the cyborg as fast as it could handle.

When the edge of the Ural Mountains appeared in front of them, Dr. Steiner breathed a sigh of relief. No towns or villages were within sight. He could surrender himself and his creation to their fate.

He slowed Apollyon down until it remained stationary as it hovered several thousand feet in the air. The dragon gave a weary moan of grinding gears and sputtering electricity. Dr. Steiner could empathize. He slumped in the dragon's hand, his mind emptying of circuitry controls and system commands. He thought of his daughter and hoped she was safe.

The encasing on the cold fusion reactor was splintering. As the sound of each crack echoed in his ears, Dr. Steiner knew his life was almost over. *What was it all for?* he wondered. *My life, my work...all wasted on a death machine.* He thought again of Eva. *Maybe she will turn out to be a better scientist than I ever was. Perhaps she will succeed where I have failed and will make the world a better place. May it be so, dear God. And please have mercy on my soul.*

A bright light enveloped the doctor, and he saw nothing more.

EPILOGUE

The Apollyon Incident sent shockwaves around the globe. Millions of people on both sides of the war were horrified at the destruction the cyborg had caused and at how close it had come to wreaking havoc on the rest of the world. Life seemed to stop for many of the citizens of Earth as they tried to grasp the enormity of what had happened.

The effects on the war were immediate. Having invested heavy amounts of military funds into the annihilated cybernetic dragon, the American Alliance called for a ceasefire rather than a surrender. Russia, with its government in shambles and military severely disabled, had no choice but to agree. China, its Coalition partner, would only agree to the ceasefire if the Alliance made certain concessions. Feeling global pressure to end the war peacefully and not finding anything unreasonable in China's conditions, the American Alliance agreed. Thus an uneasy time of peace began.

The evils and merits of the Rex-1 operation were debated for decades to come. Some claimed that the project had accomplished exactly what it had set out to do: a quick end to the war. Others argued that the cost of lives and risk to global safety had been far too high. The durability of the peaceful ceasefire was also brought into question. No one could predict what consequences the Incident would have on the nations' relations in the years to come.

But of all the stories that emerged from the history of the Apollyon Incident, one provided more astonishment and hope than any other. It was said that two years after the cyborg's attack, a beautiful American scientist and a young, retired Russian soldier who had met each other on the battlefield of Moscow were happily married. Their union, the culmination of the most unlikely of romances, made headline news across the globe. Soon afterwards, they partnered with a another survivor of the Incident, a Japanese-American aviator, to form the Steiner Memorial Peace Foundation, an organization dedicated to finding scientific solutions to issues that threatened conflict between the nations. The couple remained public figures for many years, a living testament to the power of love prevailing over chaos.

HOUSE OF THE LIVING
BY NICK HAYDEN

Sometime late 2012, Nathan and I challenged each other to write a short story based in one of the other writer's worlds. I chose the world of *Destroyer* for my story. My wife had written the second part of the novel, and I had brainstormed with her about it. I remembered throwing out ideas about the crystals that preserved the T-Rex. She decided not to go that angle, but the potential of "extraterrestrial crystals" stayed with me.

The trick, of course, was deciding how to make a story about alien crystals that keep flesh from decaying dramatic.

This is my answer. I hope you enjoy.

Nick Hayden
June 2014

My grandmother had this room she sealed off from the rest of the house. I saw it only once or twice. The furniture was covered in plastic. There were mothballs in the drawers. And I remember a faint layer of dust, like a powdering of snow, so ancient that it still held footprints from years before.

"Get away from that door!" she scolded the first time I peeked in. I was too young and frightened to ask why.

I remember how it smelled when I first stepped into the chamber—like grandmother's house. We had on our gear, and we swept our lights through the newly unearthed expanse, deep in the cave.

I remember watching the beam of my light pass over the carcass without really understanding what I was seeing. Even after I saw, I did not believe. A few splinter-sized shards of crystal unknown to the scientific community had come to us, delivered by the strange chances that mark so many discoveries. We hoped to locate more.

We did not expect to find the body of a T-Rex.

An intact skeleton is unheard of in paleontology. This was not a skeleton. It was a corpse, flesh still flushed with blood. We approached in fear and disbelief, believing it might wake. But, of course, it had to be dead.

We were rational men; we still feared, irrationally, the unknown.

I remember the night before I married, I sensed a gulf about to open before me. I lay in bed, unable to sleep, feeling as if a pit were swallowing me. I told myself it was my imagination. It was cold feet. Becky loved me, and I thought it fine to spend my life with her.

Life was ending, in a way. That's how I explained it to myself. I had felt my freedom slowly slipping from me. Becky wanted to watch a movie on Saturday night or she wanted to play a game of Monopoly on Thursday. It wasn't much. I loved her. That was just how life was going to be now, a new sort of life

I sank into the pit in my dreams, and woke disconcerted, as if something had been chasing me.

The dinosaur was dead, but preserved as if alive. Perfectly preserved. Better preserved than the Declaration of Independence, and millions of years older.

Dorian, as the T-Rex was named, was studied as a whole and then chopped into pieces, like that story in the Bible. No one ever talks about that story. A woman's raped and killed and her master, who had not lifted a finger to help, cuts her into twelve pieces and sends a body part to each tribe of Israel to decry that such evil existed in the Holy Land.

Perhaps there was evil in Dorian; Moscow certainly thought so by the time the war ended so strangely. It was none of my concern. My studies did not relate to the T-Rex.

Others claimed the crystals were evil, but that was later.

I attended Dr. Kiefer Steiner's memorial service, the one they held in the States after all the hubbub concerning the Apollyon Incident died down. Dr. Steiner was a respected colleague, if not exactly a friend.

There was no body. I like it best that way. A corpse is worse than a skeleton; a skeleton is bereft of something tangible, a corpse of something essential but elusive. Death is more palpable without the body. You can pretend the person has simply disappeared, like a character on a show that's been canceled, stuck in an eternal present you'll revisit someday.

I remember one of our mutual acquaintances complaining afterwards, as we professionals gathered to chat outside the funeral home. "You hear what people say. They say he deserved his end because he tried to play God."

We created God in the first place, I thought. He's the image we created for ourselves, the aspiration of intelligent man, the goal of evolution. I said, "Of course he played God. What else are we supposed to do? Play monkey?"

I remember the exact moment—it was at Angelo's. I had the ziti al forno. Becky was talking about her day. I added comments about my own. I remember mentioning an incident that had happened during lunch, how the electricity went off for a moment and ruined Greg's computations. I don't remember what she said.

Somewhere beneath her words was an unspoken emotion. I sensed it first when we ordered. It lurked beneath our meal, silent. I think if I would have asked, she would have come out with it, whatever it was.

I pressed on, talking now of politics.

The crystals were not terrestrial in origin. That was obvious from the start. They emitted an energy that had preserved a T-Rex for millions of years. The applications of such a process, if harnessed, were innumerable.

Such a process should also be impossible.

Entropy is the central truth of the universe. Everything runs down to darkness and chaos and nothing. Everything decays and dies. The T-Rex had not; though dead, it remained as if breath had just left it.

I remember Becky crying over the phone. I didn't understand what she was saying at first. She had stopped her pills without telling me, conceived without telling me, and now what might have been life was gone. She was convinced she had lost it, though she couldn't have been more than 6 or 7 weeks.

"Why? Why did it happen?"

She needed something, someone to blame so she could make sense of it. I understood that. But my brain would not absorb what had happened. She seemed a different person than I had left that morning, as if she'd lived a whole life in the hours of my absence. I spoke like a scientist: "Some abnormality must have affected the fetus. The body rejected it." There was no one to blame.

She hung up, and I could not help but feel relief.

When I first examined the lattice of the crystals, I stared and tried to comprehend.

There is an order in nature, in the arrangement of atoms and the structure of matter. But I did not see the regular, geometric pattern I expected; I saw a jungle.

Filaments—fibrous vines—interwoven and splayed and twisted, forming a mass of tangles. Somehow, on the macro level, the structure resembled crystal, the convolutions resolving into order just as in those posters where a thousand distinct pictures form a single large design. Except this was like taking a thousand paint splattered canvases and constructing the ceiling of Sistine Chapel.

In the early days, we wore containment suits when studying the crystals. I remember the hassle of putting the thing on. We laughed; we looked like aliens ourselves, and we took such pains to protect ourselves from what had preserved almost-life for millions of years.

We exposed mice to the crystals. We found no change in them until death. Then they remained as if in stasis. We had one cage where live specimens routinely tried to interact with a mouse that had died three years previously beneath the gaze of the crystals.

When I was twenty-one, I got the call that my mother had been in an accident. I hadn't more than that to go on, but I knew immediately that she had died. It was 9:24pm when I received the call. I remember looking at my phone just before answering.

It seems that the mind isn't designed to accept death. For months afterward, when I called home, I expected her voice instead of dad's. I discovered the newest book by her favorite author and wanted to tell her. Even twenty years later, I found myself looking at the date on the calendar and remembering, suddenly, that this was the day she died.

We never found another crystal deposit. The NASA people determined the size and date of the meteor that had brought them to earth, even calculated the patch of sky it originated from. They never discovered a life-sustaining planet in that direction, but they kept looking.

Eventually, researchers in every major country managed to get a hold of a few shards of the original collection. My own access was limited. I had been privy to their discovery, and I was respected in my circles, but my circles were small, and after the Apollyon Incident, I didn't care to be in the spotlight.

I remember reading, some time after those early days, the journal that put forth the first solid hypothesis on the structure and purpose of the crystals.

"I don't understand." She was trying to, but I was talking fast and she had been engaged in one of her books moments before. "Brain tissue?"

She looked old and tired. I remember thinking that when I paused. We had never had children, and she read voraciously, three or four books a week despite work. And I let her be.

"No, not exactly. I'm not explaining it correctly. You know how DNA works?"

"A double helix or something, right?"

"A twisted strand of information. Compact. Remarkably efficient. Just like a computer stores information in ones and zeroes. It's data. If we begin to examine it with information theory—"

"I still don't understand. Everyone's known that. You told me something like that before."

"I said it had order, that it had to mean something. Of course it has to mean something. It looks random, but it couldn't be. The researcher who wrote the paper is a neurologist. He points out very convincing points of similarities between the brain's make-up and the crystal's internal structure. Not the shape, but the arrangement and the way the energy pulses through the lattice—like brain waves."

She wasn't impressed. It was alien; she expected anything, and so the revelation seemed anticlimactic. She read books, and everything did happen in books. But in real life, not everything was possible.

Was it an alien brain we had carved up and scattered across the globe? Was it a collective of minds? A backup of some consciousness long dead? An artificial lifeform?

Whatever it was, it was immeasurably complex and oddly powerful. The energy it gave off was a byproduct of what we now considered a thought process or a simulation of thought. Perhaps the energy was a sort of telepathy or speech we could not understand.

I never saw a picture or the footage, but I imagined it vividly. Dr. Lily Chen, mid-40s, sitting unprotected beneath the crystals, leaning her head against the sharp surface of one. Waiting, willing, summoning—nothing. I don't know how often she had tried to communicate in this way; I don't know what motivated her. Afterward, many tried to extrapolate from earlier records.

That day, she'd added something special. Some sort of antiemetic plus pentobarbital. In a bit, she begins to become drowsy. She leans her head against the crystal, as always. Her eyes close, willing, summoning....

When her lab assistant finds her, she looks asleep. A dribble of blood hangs on her forehead where the pressure against a shard has cut her. She is dead, but not quite. She is stuck in the moment of death.

They do not move her. For a week, they run tests, until they can no longer keep her death a secret.

I see her still, asleep, red blood upon her forehead.

I think my wife knows I sometimes see other women. I suspect she sees other men, if not in real life, then in her books. I cannot compete with her book-men. And though they are fictional, I sometimes think they are more real to her than I am. She peeks in at their seeming lives, returning again and again to re-read the same dead words that hold the verisimilitude of life.

We create our realities. We choose what to allow and what to ignore. The brain that processes concrete surroundings processes the abstractions of imagination. All great art began within and was ushered out into the physical world by artists. Was their art less real before it was created? Let there be light—and there was.

I do not blame her for her incorporeal world. Myself, maybe, but not her.

I remember when I first made contact. I was speaking to it. It was a habit I had formed from the beginning, like when one talks to a dog or a baby not expecting it to understand. After discovering what it might be, I talked more deliberately, hoping the mind (or minds) within would hear and, over time, come to understand.

For years, nothing happened. Even as I continued with more pressing research, I made time each week to visit. It was a nearly religious experience for me—a ritual cleansing to prepare myself, then a prayer in the confessional booth. Whenever I began to grow self-conscious of my time with the crystals, I reminded myself of my scientific purpose.

It had been a hard week. My father had called and told me he'd been diagnosed with prostate cancer. I'd feared, irrationally, something like this for the last 25 years, ever since my mom died. I told the crystals what I felt, how I was afraid of death.

And they spoke to me.

My dad reacted badly to the news of cancer; he became a Christian. He threw himself into it wholeheartedly, and I always thought of it as an act of desperation.

One day when we met for supper he tried to convert me. He looked horrible. The chemo had ravaged him. He had not lived a particularly clean life—alcohol, gambling, maybe drugs, all at one time or another. I don't know what all. I didn't ask. It went in phases like everything with him. For seven months, he went vegan.

"Do you remember when you were nine," he said after he tried to explain the wonders of the Godhead, "and you woke up screaming? Do you remember that?"

I did.

"You'd had a nightmare about the end of the universe. Darkness, you kept saying between tears. Darkness and nothingness forever. It really affected you. I remember it because it affected me, too. You always had a mind that fixated on the big things. Small things, at least if they were small to you, didn't matter."

I thought he was going to try the "small things do matter" route. It wouldn't be the first time.

"Do you know what the Bible says?" he continued. He was completely earnest. "'I am making everything new.' And somewhere, I forget where, it talks about the indestructible life of Jesus. There's this sense of life bubbling up, unstoppable, and I thought of your nightmare and decided I needed to tell you. Life everlasting."

There was nothing to say to that. It was another story, a variation of what occupied the hours of Becky's life, one of a million realities created and traded every day. Not my reality. I tried to smile and said, "Thank you, dad."

When they spoke to me, they did not use words. It was a vision. It passed through my mind like a nightmare—a deep purple sky, cracked swollen land, a touch upon me like a finger of fire; deep, twisting caverns;

102

rough, reverent motion deep in the earth; and fear, fear so thick and dull it made me want to vomit.

It is hard for me to detail my experience in better terms. An alien mind touched me and what little I could fathom were like snapshots strung haphazardly together.

I do not think it meant to communicate with me, that it had any true interest in my being. I think this because I understood its fear—the gnawing anxiety of a life slipping away to no purpose, to no end, to dust and darkness. We shared this fear, and when it sensed it in me, it searched me out, so that it wasn't alone.

I kissed my wife that night and tried to talk to her, but I was out of practice and she had long ago hidden her self from me. I sat up, restless, useless, late into the night, like Scrooge visited by his ghosts and unable to act on his newfound convictions.

And what were my convictions? Nothing, just emotion, a deep unsettledness, a desperate need to connect with someone else who understood.

It frightened me that I had made contact with an alien life, and it held no answers. It was as lost as I was.

I sought out Dr. Phillip Snyder, who had made recent advances in understanding the crystals' energy signal. I flew to California to have dinner with him, saying I wished to share research.

He was a tall, thick man, built like an athlete. He had piercing, calculating eyes. After small talk and appetizers, I told him of my experience.

I remember his stern, thoughtful face. I felt compelled to add: "It's the truth."

"What do they want?" He did not seem to be mocking me.

"I don't know. I don't understand most of what I saw. But I know it's not a computer, not an artificial intelligence. They are in there. I don't think they know where they are or even that something exists outside of their...surroundings."

"Try contacting them again. I need more information."

"It was an accident. I've tried again. I don't think they want to communicate."

"So, you can guess what they don't want? You connected with it, it seems. If what you say happened is true, it is likely you understand them subconsciously. Don't think. Just answer. What do they want?"

"Not to die."

A hotel room is a lonely place. When it is dark and the streets below are full of cars and unknown faces, when the room is too cold and your few belongings are splayed around your carry-on, you live in an island of reality. You can imagine all sorts of petty fantasies or mope in vague anxieties. The TV whitters away, munching down time. You want to call someone; you hope for a knock at the door and a smile; you raid the vending machine for encouragement.

This is life.

Dr. Snyder invited me back, this time to his lab. He shook my hand with his strong grip and explained what he planned to do and my role in it.

So I sat in a chair, strapped in case I lost consciousness, and tried to feel out the alien mind. It was useless, I knew, and I could not speak to them without embarrassment because he was observing me. But he ran his tests, recording my brainwaves alongside the crystals' energy readings.

Then he began to smash the crystals to powder.

He had a machine that did it, and I knew he used it reluctantly, but he was convinced that if I was right, if the aliens didn't want to die, then threatening the safety of their consciousness was the best way to make them show themselves.

I remember that first blow, the crack. I began to cry. I didn't want to, but the emotion hit me powerfully. We were murdering them, or what was left of them. They were terrified of the emptiness beyond.

"Stop!" I cried out. Tears streamed down my face. "Stop!" Deep terror assailed me; my vision darkened. I don't know how much of it was my doing, how much was theirs.

When I recovered, Dr. Snyder was reviewing the data. "Fascinating."

"I am the resurrection and the life."

I tried not to cry at my father's funeral. It had been expected. It was the way of all life. Everyone lost their father eventually.
I didn't miss him yet; I hadn't time for that. But his body in the coffin was a shell; he had gone. Had he gone to heaven—as he had believed at the end?

I knew he was gone. And he wasn't coming back. "He's in a better place," they tried to tell me.

I wanted to believe what the preacher preached. But I couldn't. I wouldn't. I don't know why. Sometimes I wonder: is it because I would have to give up my fear, give up everything? To believe, I'd have to choose a story that wasn't mine.

Everyone believes some story, but my faith in entropy was stronger than my faith in God.

Somehow, I didn't hear about it until it was in the regular media. In journals, researchers had begun to apply the crystals' energy in experimental ways, but this went way beyond laboratory fiddling. In Washington state, the first House of the Living opened. An alternate to assisted suicide, terminally ill patients could be preserved until such a time as a cure might be found. All they need do is sit near the crystals, let themselves be injected with a lethal substance and let the preserving power of the crystals do its work. The humane alternative, the news declared.

Years later, I toured one of these facilities. It had dozens of rooms filled with hundreds of bodies, a city of people frozen in time, their bodies full of almost-vitality—a building of living cadavers.

I studied Dr. Snyder's analysis obsessively. He was onto something. His recording of the energy signatures were filtered through the latest advances in neurobiology. They bore the signs of dream-state thought, but with such noise that it was nearly indistinguishable, like a picture glimpsed through a snowstorm or a melody drowned in static.

I suggested running Dr. Lily Chen's crystals through his scheme. That was my contribution. He gave me a copy of the results, but he discovered the vital piece before I did and so his name is known and mine is not.

"Invasion of the Brain Snatchers" became the Internet headline, but the truth was far more encouraging. We found Dr. Chen's brainwave in the noise of the crystals. It still existed within. And the noise—the thoughts of thousands of aliens dreaming.

I never worried about my wife leaving me; she had abandoned the marriage long before, but we were both too afraid to end it. We grew old together. She had a stroke. She never recovered.

I had never been so lonely.

I had made the decision years before. Once she was gone, nothing held me back but my own fear. I made my appointment and arrived at the local House of the Living fifteen minutes early.

"Reason for stasis?" the Life Counselor asked.

"Genetic predisposition to prostate cancer." They could (and would) verify this against my genetic profile.

The requirements had lessened considerably over the years, but technically, it was against policy to let a young, healthy person into stasis. Cost was the greater limiter, though a surge of religious fundamentalism also discouraged a percentage of the population. But I had the money. I'd made monthly deposits against this day.

I signed the paperwork and went through the legally required video warnings. "This way please."

The room she led me to was already occupied. A young man, no older than 30, sat in the provided recliner. It was extended nearly horizontal. A patch of crystal rested against his forehead. His face was almost serene, but there was a tension about the eyes, a slackness about the jaw….

"I apologize, sir. This room is in use." My nurse was angry. Someone would get a lecture. "We'll use Room 5B."

She explained the process briskly, reiterating what I had already read and watched. "Is there anything you would like? Our in-house restaurant comes highly recommended, and we offer other services as well. We only ask you be done in two hours, or else we will ask you to leave, no refunds."

"I'm fine. Thank you."

"Sweet dreams." She closed the door.

I sat in the chair and tried not to consider too deeply her final words. This wasn't dying—but what was it exactly? We still didn't know. They dream, people claimed. Eternal dreams, like happily ever after. But I wondered sometimes. The aliens had been full of fear. If the brain was absorbed into the lattice, how did it exist? Did it continue to create and ponder, or was it static, simply a copy of what existed at the time of transfer, a series of memories jumbled together, vividly remembered and eternally relived?

I closed my eyes and reclined the chair. With one press of the button, the crystal would lower until its cool surface touched my head. This was the end—no, not the end. Death was the end. This—it wasn't death. It was something else.

I pressed the button. I felt the sharp edges through my thin hair. The room began to fill with gas (my choice), silently, edging me to death's door.

And I began to remember….

ACKNOWLEDGMENTS

This novella, while short, was a labor of love for us, and it couldn't have been written without our creative community and literary influences.

First, a big shout-out to this story's initial inspirations: *Frankenstein* by Mary Shelly and the films *Gojira* (*Godzilla*, 1954) and *Cloverfield*, tales that proved (giant) monster stories can have great characters and themes.

A huge thank you to Derailed Trains of Thought, the "unofficial" writers' club of Taylor University Fort Wayne. Not only were you the creative community we needed to hone our crafts, but you contributed to the creation of this novella through the year-long "Pulp Fiction Project," which this was part of. We can't wait to see those other pulp stories get published!

Nick Hayden, Natasha's husband and the club's "founder" and leader. Thank you for directing us to Lulu and Smashwords as avenues for the first printing of this book and for all your help with layout and formatting.

Speaking of Lulu and Smashwords, thank you for providing the first means to share this story with readers. Without you, this book may have not seen the light of day.

Thanks to CreateSpace for providing the means for publishing this deluxe edition of the novella.

A big thank to J.D, Lees, editor of the Godzilla fanzine, *G-Fan*, for posting the want ad that led us to our cover artist.

About that cover artist: thank you so much, Tyler Sowles, for your awesome work creating the gorgeous oil painting that adorns this book's front cover. We would love to work with you again!

Last but certainly not least, all glory must go to Jesus Christ for blessing us with talent and a story to tell. Amen!

ABOUT THE AUTHORS

Nathan Marchand is a freelance writer, avid storyteller, and available bachelor. He was a reporter for the *Bluffton News-Banner*, and now writes about Narnia, superheroes, and Star Trek for www.Examiner.com and all things geeky for *GigaGeek Magazine*. His first novel, *Pandora's Box*, was published in 2010. His website is www.nathanjsmarchand.com. He freely admits Godzilla movies are his guilty pleasure.

Natasha Hayden is a full-time mom and wife with a passion for stories, both the ones she reads and those she writes. She reviews the latest in young adult fiction on her blog natashasshelf.blogspot.com. She doesn't know how she got roped into contributing to a monster story but is glad she had the opportunity to help create the in-depth kind of characters she loves in the midst of such chaos. She could be bribed into doing it again.

Timothy Deal is a writer and filmmaker whose love of all types of storytelling sometimes gets him buried in project ideas. He is currently putting his M.A. in Cinema-Television to work as a freelance videographer and continues to co-host (with Nick Hayden) a storytelling podcast at derailedtrainsofthought.blogspot.com. He hopes to get to some of the other projects on his list while avoiding digging up any frozen dinosaur remains.

Nick Hayden is married to his lovely wife Natasha and is father to his wonderful children Fyodor (no, we are not Russian) and Serenity. Sometimes Nick really loves to write. Sometimes, he prefers to dream about writing. Most times, he enjoys reading things he's already written.
Above all, Nick hopes that something he writes will inspire you, entertain you, make you think, or simply make you smile. If not, he supposes he'll have to keep at it until something does. His website is www.worksofnick.com.

ALSO BY THE AUTHORS

Pandora's Box
by Nathan Marchand
(published by Absolute Xpress, an imprint of EDGE
Science Fiction and Fantasy. Available on Amazon)

The Day After
by Nathan Marchand, Natasha Hayden, Nick Hayden,
and Keith Osmun
(Available from Amazon and www.Smashwords.com)

The Story Project: The Journals - Year 1
by Natasha Hayden, Timothy Deal, Nick Hayden, and
others
(Available from Amazon and www.Smashwords.com)

The Story Project: The Journals – Year 2
by Natasha Hayden, Timothy Deal, Nick Hayden and
others
(Available from Amazon and www.Smashwords.com)

Children of the Wells: Bron and Calea, Vol. 1
by Nick Hayden and Laura Fischer
(Available from Amazon and
www.ChildrenoftheWells.com)

Children of the Wells: Jaysynn, Vol. 1
by Nathan Marchand, John Bahler, and Timothy Deal
(Available from Amazon and
www.ChildrenoftheWells.com)

Made in the USA
Lexington, KY
02 September 2017